WORKBOOK PRESS LLC
187 E Warm Springs Rd
Suite B285 Las Vegas NV 89119 USA

Website: https://workbookpress.com/
Hotline: 1-888-818-4856
Email: admin@workbookpress.com

Ordering Information:
Quantity sales. Special discounts are available on quantity purchases by corporations, associations, and others. For details, contact the publisher at the address above.

ISBN-13:   978-1-963718-88-1 Paperback Version
                  978-1-963718-89-8 Digital Version

PUB. DATE: 7/19/2024

GUANAJA DEFENSE

MODERN DAY WAR FOR THE BAY ISLANDS

By Lance Starr

BOOK ONE

PROLOGUE

Hostage Hotel: Emergence Of Rage

We received a worried call from Captain Brearly. Five people from the Artificial Island were barricaded in the newer Cartel hotel in Orilla. Three women and two guys. Two mature women tourists and a nineteen-year-old girl were trapped.

Vanna and I hopped on our Starr resort security boat and headed over to Brearly's island on-board office. He was fuming and in distress. He was responsible and if the worst happened, he would be looking for a much less lucrative job. Someone hiding in a towel closet was calling on a cell phone.

I wasn't comfortable becoming the de-facto cop of the Bay Islands. Vanna and I had discussed it in our after-love bubble. We were hoping Brearly, with strong backup resources, would shoulder it. Unfortunately, this wasn't his kind of warfare. His tactics had already put people in the town hospital. The people had no other alternatives, and I couldn't get him to read "tactics of the Blue Coats in the Revolutionary War". Vanna and I went, hoping to be tactical advisors.

The situation was ten in the hotel. Five from the island. Five of the hotel staff pushed dressers and couches against the doors. One staff member had a double-barrel shotgun. Eight cartel thugs outside swearing and threatening, fully armed. U.S. White Supremacists seconded by the drug cartel brandishing American assault weapons.

Brearly reached to call his Black Private SWAT helicopters. Vanna and I stopped him.

"If these guys hear rotors, they'll shoot their way in. They know that SWAT will be their end. You'll lose people, yours and others. The thugs will be drinking hard tonight. They'll be planning to go in tomorrow, salivating about the nineteen-year-old girl. We have time and can head this off tonight. Give us three hours and we'll end it."

Vanna and I were back in the fight. Our tactics are not foolproof, but more efficient, and field-tested.

Lance deploys, "Octavio, where are you, over?"

"Birdcage, I'm empty, west of your Guanaja, resort lights in the distance. Where are you? Over."

"We're on the Artificial Island with the Captain, the problem is on Orilla. I need you and your cruiser tonight, not urgently. Come to Orilla and anchor by the gravel airport by 2 a.m. Keep the sodium lights off unless I say differently. We have some artificial island clients in the new hotel under siege by some Bay Island Drug gang, seconded by Midwest American White Supremacists. Out."

Lance briefs, "Captain Brearly, we're going to slip in behind them and take them down while they're drunk. Do you have another diver in your security crew?"

"Lance, I'm sorry. I've only trained sports divers, nothing like the professionals you need. Are you sure you don't want chopper support?"

"Ok, Brearly, put a chopper under my control, or yours, following my orders. That is non-negotiable; no staggered involvement by the U.S. drone base. For the moment, have them aloft, down-wind west of Orilla out of hearing. Be aware, I have dear life-long friends working to avoid choppers on scene until after the action goes down. I don't want anybody stopping, moving, or starting carefully orchestrated movements. Nobody is going to get killed in my group from reeling government rules of engagement or hunches of an incompetent self-aggrandizing commander-in-chief."

Brearly, "OK, Lance, we are in your waters, my career is hanging on your abilities."

Lance re-directs, "Roberto, where are you?"

"Birdcage, I'm floating amongst my shrimp encouraging them to reproduce. You are calling me for something more complicated than shrimp-seduction. Over?"

"We have a siege on the new hotel on Orilla. There are no cartel police there, ever. Nor would they help unless bribed. You know this better than I. We can head this off but have to do it tonight. We need another diver. How far away are you? Over."

"If absolutely necessary, I'm on the southwest peninsula of Roaban, in my shrimp farm. Over."

"Roberto, several of these captives are from the Artificial Island, some women, and one young one. I tried to get a diver from there but they have none. They want to have their rental SWAT do a frontal deluge. I convinced them they'll lose tourists. The captain, Brearly, 'Black Bird', confirms via his drone who the thugs are and they are outside drinking heavily. What White Supremacists are doing supporting brown thugs shows how badly their NRA leaders have corrupted their treasury. If we can get in there tonight, we'll save tourist lives. Tourists are the priority."

"Roberto, Vanna and I are here. Vanna is probably worth two of us; we need another diver to even the odds. We're going back to the resort to get armament. If you have a metal jacket and can deal with it and a black wetsuit, wear it. We can't use grenades unless they are tossed outside of the building. Bring a couple. Maybe we can use them campfire-side. We'll bring two RPGs. Close-in use may be dangerous to tourists facing ransom or death. Bring your sound suppressed rifles and pistols. We'll meet at the airport at 2 am. Maximum surprise critical!"

Roberto answers, "I'll come. Of course. Have you considered Bucky. He could run down the road from the town and over the bogs without floundering. I can pick him up and drop him at the airport with something of the clothes any of those terrorists are wearing. He'll smell and track them in 15 minutes. We need to get there first to hold him. Rather than a frontal attack from the water which the thugs surely expect, he can plow the path open from the land side and we'll clean up. Over"

Lance, "Ok, bring Bucky. Octavio will be at the airport. I think we need to hold him back for clean-up. He's heavily armed and speed of lightning on the water. He can get there in a minute and a half if necessary. We're heading back to the resort. Over."

"Be there at two. Roberto, out."

Vanna and I dressed in black rubber with cork black eyes; her blonde hair up and hidden. We loaded the armaments in our security boat changing the engine to electric.

"Black Bird, we're heading out. Any new drone information?"

Brearly, "Bird cage, the manager of the hotel called, in tears. He escaped out the back and now feels he was a coward. He confirms five friendlies and five staff plus himself. We now know the guests are in the conference room on the west side of reception, ground floor. The front door, water side, is barred. The staff were brave, but there are many windows right into reception. Bogies are well-armed. Over"

Birdcage back, "tell the owner to send a staff member via the basement to the airport. He'll have to wade through muck. We'll arm him and he can gain some advantage for us from the basement. The drunks may well be unaware of that. We'll give him a sound suppressed pistol. He should wait till he hears our rifles or a grenade before attacking. His cover is not more important than his life. Tell him to duck first and run if seen."

"Black Bird, can you get a description of the room arrangement down-stairs and main floor? Nobody here has ever been there."

"I'll be right back birdcage. Over."

We all arrived at the airport at 2 a.m. There are few flights to this place even during heavy season. Unspoiled reefs exist that I take the advanced groups to visit. We avoid walking up on the island due to lack of sanitary conditions.

Octavio was last in, running low rpms to stay quiet. Vanna had made a rough sketch based on the hotel manager's description. We forwarded them to Brearly and poured over them to make an attack plan.

We couldn't bring the electric motor closer than a half kilometer. We'd have to swim, quietly, the remainder. We put arms in a black inner tube to keep them accessible and dry. The swim was no challenge to any of us after all the dives we led. Roberto had his bullet proof half-vest under good control as did Vanna and I. No lead weights needed tonight.

Closer to the target, there were bogs full of garbage we had to avoid. The shore was ragged, sometimes three feet deep, sometimes over our heads. On the smelling, crusty shore, Bucky was forced, because of the muck, to jump from bog to bog for every movement forward. He arrived earlier than anticipated and had to hide in the cat-tails until I whistled.

Surely a disgusting place for a beach. For a hotel, as well. More the question why the cartel wanted to mess with it. Probably some bad blood between the owner and the Don J. Mondo, mafia chief; role model for recent U.S. leadership. Maybe the maximum stay was fifteen days.

I clicked twice on my mic to get a response the staff boy was back and in a safe location. Two clicks back confirmed. Bucky was chomping at the proverbial bit. I couldn't send him in advance if we should use hand grenades.

"Take your fins off, keep your booties on. Quietly. There isn't much drunken movement. If we lose surprise, we lose tourist lives. Do you count 8 around the fire?"

Vanna, quiet whisper, "No, hold off, we have only seven. Don't move. Wait."

In two minutes one of the criminals came around the west side of the building zipping his pants up. He'd been dangerously close to the conference room windows. There was quiet, controlling sobs.

Lance directed, "Let him sit down, wait two beats and Roberto, throw the grenade in. Getting them, all here will guarantee safety for the tourists. Now!"

The grenade cracked. Two thugs survived or were wounded.

I whistled Bucky.

One thug ducked around where the other had peed. Vanna took one step to the side and double-tap, before he could access the conference room window. The other dived through the reception window trying to get to his feet and fire through the conference room door. He raised his U.S. assault weapon, and Bucky took him by the neck. I didn't hear the 'pfft' of the staff boy's suppressed pistol, the thug's ear erupted. Bucky recoiled back out the window.

Suddenly it was quiet. Sniffles and soft cries from inside. Roberto quickly checked the receivers of the grenade. No movement. Guns removed, no life.

"Octavio, with mask on, come in stat."

He got there, revved, in only a minute.

Lance continued, "Roberto, go in and keep the tourists in that room. Don't let them see us. Put on a mask. Limit voice. If they get drunk and try to describe us, I want them to be wrong."

"Vanna, Octavio, go back and get our security boat. I don't want blood on your new cruiser."

"Lance?"

The manager sidled in and I put him soundly back with the

tourists. I asked the name of the staff boy who'd saved the group at the end. He stepped out; name was Jesus. With a few words, I enthused about how brave he'd been and saved lives. I asked him to look for Railroad Juan next he was in Cuenca. He returned the pistol. I sent him back with the tourists. I waited with my mask to carry away the grisly remains.

"Black bird, this is Birdcage. It's over, your people are not injured. Send a helicopter to pick them up? Nobody needs to know our names."

Brearly in relief, "Dam it, yes, on the way, Birdcage. Out!"

. . . .

IN SHORT, over the millennia, South and Central America were constantly clashing cultures. Simon Bolivar appeared on the scene and for a few years brought peace. Since his time, things have plunged adding Pirate Drug Cartels and Coyotes guiding drugs and individuals from countries with failed governments. Next door the big U.S. government siphoning money from Cartels and mixing the drugs seriously with "Lobbying" complicated the attacks. Although this narrative is fiction, elements of it exist and burst onto the world via Trump immigration cages and mountains of bribery and corruption. The hope of having another "Simon Bolivar is sadly dim. Lance Starr and Vanna Richards try to leave a hopeful mark.

MODERN DAY WAR
FOR THE BAY ISLANDS

Lance's Caribbean Central Scuba Operation

The Starr Resort, Guanaja

Book One: CONCEPT AND CREATION

CHAPTER 1

Fifteen Years Earlier-Midwest University Graduation

My early life was in the water. From swimming exhaustingly around an old rusted raft chasing friends, to ski tricks, rescue; scuba diving, I developed as an Alpha Male. That provided draw in staffing, diving and hosting generally well-to-do guests in the Bay Islands.

Scuba training had to go on hold. I was in a land-locked University eventually gaining an MS in Developmental and Marine Engineering in fresh water. I gained a room-mate, Greg, who was the imaginative designer, the one who could see most any object and find an improvement. To imagine building from scratch took him mentally away. We couldn't rouse him, though he was sitting right there. He responded like an eidetic reader remembering everything.

Greg and I shared the normal bed-on-opposite walls dorm room. Tight for trysting and too small for a party. Across the hall lived Roberto Fernandez, a Honduran with a well-to-do father. Fernandez was warm and cooperative with the largest room in that dorm. He would conveniently be out of suite if Greg or I were 'entertaining'. Co-ED was not an issue in Grad School. Roberto was in for a Masters in Marine Engineering/ Minor in Sea Mammal Health.

Greg married sooner than he had ever projected. She was besides beautiful, a Materials Engineer in her own right. We, the threesome, with d' Artagnan across the hall were the classic team.

When Greg innovated a new Mercedes dashboard, all available preset digital communication and control technologies within arms-reach, I built it. Knowing the red-neck administration tendencies, Cheryl agreed as eye candy. We visited the Mercedes offices in the mid-west. They said they would give us a call. We immediately patented it. Not going to fall for that trap. We were busy as we waited. Greg's mind would never stop. I had a dream about making a life around the sea: a scuba, water skiing and parasailing resort. That's what I did. Greg and Cheryl weren't aficionados of the salt. They shared in the one-million-dollar sale of the patent from Mercedes. My share avoided debt to my parents and smaller investors in financing the Starr Scuba Resort. It extended the size of the resort to be.

In the same time frame, my spring break took me south, not to Florida. The Bay Islands of Honduras were beginning to develop, I thought. The fellow graduate student across the corridor providing fun for us, Honduran, talked up the Salva Vida beer. Well connected. He joined me and I watched him buy a shrimp farm and a "Swim with the Dolphins" show he would develop after next year's graduation. Visiting him on the Big Island, Roaban, he recalled my dreaming in our cups at the Steel Rail bar at school. I didn't have to tell him what I was looking for.

Knowing I was coming, Roberto had looked around for a location for my water resort. It could be on the hilly north side of the Island of Guanaja. We visited. We went to the lawyer he trusted. I used the patent money to avoid any large mortgage. With yearly profits, growth continued. Two years later there was a dock, five cabanas throughout the trees on the side hill, a kitchen-bar restaurant with stools and five booths. A friend from the Banana Company and Roberto with a local builder helped me construct it. The banana guy took no pay and now stays any and every time he wishes, complements.

Mercedes was very interested in Greg's knack for invention. He was very interested in who would fabricate his new ideas. That's me. Together we were brought to Germany. Greg's portion of the million dollar patent is hidden in an IRA. Greg and Cheryl located in Munich, a design center. I was further north in Frankfurt, construction and finance center. We were initially worried for what Cheryl would do. A month later we visited the military expats bar in Kaiserslautern. Two weeks later she was designing and removing military buildings in several regions of West Central Germany.

For the first two years at the resort, nobody got a vacation. We couldn't walk away. Roberto hired a day-to-day manager and found a large boat with a ramp for scuba divers. The diving business began to bloom. As time went by, the team of Greg and I blossomed with me re-designing and constructing what he imagined. I constantly created metal parts using rented ancient on-shore equipment. A hot spot was one island away. Frequently via Zoom and What's-App online specs could be accessed. Other specific engineering software was in my grasp locally or on-line. Essential shop machines came on banana boats from Gulfport, LA.

I went to Guanaja and constructed satellite access and bought a bigger generator to serve the entire site. There was one other resort on the south side of the island focused on relaxation and small glass-bottomed boat snorkeling. I was the professional scuba guy, marketing intense dives. The other resort was the drinking one, mostly in the nude. "Nude Beaches.com" Of course, I met the owner and visited her occasionally. She had a main squeeze, but hers was a body worth walking through the jungle to view. Potentially complicated, I didn't offer access to the big generator.

Occasionally a woman would come through to my resort with a dive crew, often a diver herself. A brief encounter or two developed. She went off, both of us happy.

I was succeeding working long distance, projecting in the long run I would need to be in Germany two-three months each year. This depended on Greg who was still insatiable. With Roberto's judgement and choices, the resort was well-manned, while I was away. He was marketing shrimp and "dolphin rides" at the same time, his site was only a half hour by fast boat from my resort.

There were several local men available to run the ramp boats and cook and tend bar. Dive clubs included women members and we didn't have one. We also needed to extend our marketing specifically to Europe from where we had had three walk-in groups. Our website and brochures were attracting U.S. divers. I headed to Spain to seek a potential

European Partner. Speaking decent Spanish, it was a logical first step for me.

CHAPTER TWO

First Partnership Interview and Vetting

My second semester at university, I joined the theater group. I learned and experienced acting, directing, set construction, lighting and make-up.

I went to several Zarzuela theater performances in Madrid where I had received letters of interest in the resort position. I had some additional Spanish learned at the Official School of Languages in the Moncloa suburb; enough to volunteer to join backstage of a major Zarzuela group. I chose the group of which Denya Galicia was the one paid performer. I was a complete unknown. Getting close to her to do any vetting would take patience.

At first glance, she was fit. More than that, I would need to judge her style in relationship building. Fitting into a dive operation required many elements of empathy. After the disaster of the U.S., I wasn't going to hire a husk empty of empathy as a self-proclaimed snake to work in my troop. As an ex, he was still dangerous to the country I had once been proud of. As we moved toward opening night, backstage people attended every performance and rehearsed every placement. We listened to the lovely arias over and over. Eventually we watched the choreographer enter the animation, often very suggestive, of exotics included in the dances.

CHAPTER THREE

Candidate 1: Denya Galicia, Zarzuela Icon

Denya Galicia is the lead singer and dancer in the Zarzuela troop in Madrid located several blocks east of the Plaza Del Sol. She has volume in her low alto ranges and alluring tone in her highest coloratura. She is the love interest in Zarzuela dance scenes. Other memorable features of her strong, feminine form make her the continuous lead. These strengths would transfer smoothly to resort activities.

Sitting on an actor's waiting bench behind the curtain stage left, I saw the leading woman, the first voice, and the one who was a magnetic attraction to me. She did songs only in Spanish for the shows. Back stage and at parties, she did them in English, German and French. Her languages were ideal for foreign divers. I temporarily forgot the resort interview mission.

I swooned through the first show of five each week. Her costume was transparent. There couldn't exist a more stunning form on a woman. From her toned booty to her high thrusting breasts, I was mesmerized. She danced alone and with strong feminine men. If there were a costume, it blurred in the lights as she was whirled and lowered sensuously keeping only her tiny skirt in view.

Between wild prop changes I sat on call on the two-person bench. I was alone there and Denya came to sit, tense with anticipation. I didn't interrupt her concentration. I was their stage left every show, every exit of Denya and every entrance. There was every stage effect to embolden her essence.

On her first entrance, she moved down-stage right to sing the main theme. After the thrill of her full voice range, the audience as one was on its feet in intense applause. A stage hand up on the catwalk opened a basket. Tiny bits of reflective colors showered her. They landed and stuck to her fleecy cape, her hair and filmy arms. The magic. The cast as well as the audience bathed in it. Her passion brought tears to eyes.

Eventually she saw me there often enough to content herself that I was one of the groups. She spoke to me occasionally and listened to my "Spanish" answers and comments. I improved my Spanish language pronto. I needed more vocabulary to sense her fit for the resort.

She smiled. I held my breath. Eventually she came to the scene construction shop. I heard she was the only member of the group that was paid a living wage. The fact that she was in the construction shop frequently sealed the troop's respect. I confirmed her balance and strength for handling heavy scuba tanks. The fact that she lived, walked and breathed enriched my life. She would be an excellent candidate for Lances resort if ever she would want it.

By the time we started the fourth show, I had occasional short shallow chats. Always on the bench, I was extremely careful to check her visage before saying anything that might interrupt her character. If the view was clear, I took the opportunity to get in a little snippet about me. I hadn't gotten a formal introduction. I got a number of worthwhile smiles.

The break happened on the second night of the fourth show. She rushed into stage-left in haste, face red, tension and pain radiating from her eyes. Costumes had ignored the unbalanced flower array on the left shoulder, faulty pin, and the clip on the back of her bra was digging in. Drops of blood.

"Lance, is there a costume woman here? I'm in pain and can't reset my dress. Sorry, of course there's no woman here. Lance, can you help. I'm sure you've seen a breast before."

"Miss Galicia, I can arrange your breast faster than you

can accept a marriage proposal. She gave a start of surprise and presented me first the shoulder which I quickly reset adding comfort. She turned her back directly to me and I studied the bra strap clip. It was buried in her skin; would make a major scar if I didn't remove it vertically. To do that I had to remove one side of the bra. I told her.

"I don't want a scar. I'm on again in two minutes."

I raised the cup from the side of the puncture, removed the tension by slipping it up over the nipple, and eased the strap. I could bend the clip with my fingers. I did, reached around in front again, reset the nipple, and moved my fingers along under the strap to be certain there were no other snags. I told her she was good to go. In Spanish, of course. She turned and a flash confirmed a kiss on the cheek.

Later in the show she came my way for her last entrance. She wasn't due quickly. She had time to flash an embarrassed smile and thank me.

"Miss Galicia, you're welcome to my help anytime. Since for the moment we have broken the ice so to speak, may I be forward as to ask you to join me for a cup of coffee, or tea, or whiskey or whatever you like. I'd like to get to know the real you better and frankly would like to have you know me better, and my Caribbean resort. I know I haven't been formally presented to you. Maybe you would help with that?"

"Lance, ignoring for the moment whatever you think 'formal presentation' involves, please drop the Miss Galicia and call me Denya. This is Tuesday and maybe we can work something out. Wait for me at the stage door at the end of show and we'll discuss."

I was proud that everything was hanging beautifully and no more pain nor damage.

Waiting heart in mouth, I wished lots of people good night. Fifteen minutes passed and I stepped back inside onto stage. Not a sound. A few lights were still on. I doused them. In the shadows, I called her name twice. Nothing. I went to her dressing room. Locked.

I went back outside the door. Jilted! I had a disappointing night. The show was on again Thursday. I had props located and ready stage left.

She came around the back curtain, saw me, and said, "Oh Dios Mio, Lance!"

I turned away.

She came over and gently took my shoulder back to meet my eyes.

"Lance, please listen. I did forget, my brother was in a bicycle accident. I was called during the last scene, finished it and raced home to see what I needed to do. His lower arm was badly swollen. Definitely broken."

"A neighbor helped me get him in the car. My mom came along. I rushed, saving a 250 Euro ambulance fee which would strain my parent's finances. I went back to my apartment exhausted and slept. Now I see you. I remember our talk and our plan to meet. I am so sorry. Lance if you can forgive me, please give me your cell number. Can you forgive me? I'm sincerely interested in knowing you too."

Her resort job consideration refreshed.

"I'll survive. I'm glad your brother will be ok. The role of default mother can be stressing. When will you be available again?" I had to move this vetting along.

CHAPTER FOUR

Chinchon

"**B**esides the Zarzuela, I teach voice and piano lessons to stretch the salary beyond performing. I do reserve Sunday afternoons for social life. Few men dates are interested in Sunday evening Work-a-Holics. (In the resort, she might get less free time.) I can sometimes get away on Wednesday afternoons. Tonight is Wednesday. I have to finish up with the broken arm and transition back home. Could you be patient and meet me on Sunday?"

"What time will work?"

"I have a lesson at ten in the morning and a voice student at noon. I need a nap. Would a pick-up at 3:00 p.m. be, ok?"

"How about a date to Cinchon? It's cooler there than here. Dress with a few layers in case the sun graces us. Bye."

Visions of molded breasts, firm caress and a glorious back danced in my dreams for four nights. I rehearsed conversations, reducing idiomatic phrases, and inserted Spanish words that said it better than English.

She carried a sweater which I hoped she would never need. Come on sunshine!

I asked, "Have you been to Chinchon?"

She answered, "Yes, with my parents about ten years old. Too young to drink. I know they have anise factories along with beautiful mountain views."

"Let's walk the mountains for a while before we visit factories." This was a feint to see if she would be comfortable on a mountain trail alone with someone who had disrobed her the last time they met.

I parked at a stream coming from as far above as we could see. She had tennis shoes. We made good time with no particular place to go. We came to a granite outcrop with magnificent views both up and down the mountain. Pine trees to infinity! The landscape evolved from rugged brown where we were to dark green in the distance. Glacier boulders peppered the landscape. We sat. I had a bottle of water. I took a drink, hesitated and offered it to her. Another information-rich hint of how things are going. She took a healthy drink without hesitation, without wiping the top. She handed it back and I asked the first question. We compared the differences of numbers of names for Spanish women.

The subjects, the quick sharing, the strength to present an attitude, all endearing and resort friendly.

People came to Chinchon to set the sun and imbibe heady anise. Each Anise factory offered samples to help you choose your favorite.

We visited three. I was the driver and experienced with alcohol. She had two for each one I had. My second was watering the hedge. As we headed to the third factory, we held more than hands. The smile was flashing radiance. I could see why men hungered to have the vibrancy she could fire. Nonchalantly she'd step close to my side firmly brushing my biceps with the breast I had so gingerly saved from scarring.

At her apartment, the "buzz" was in my favor. She didn't have to close her sweater. I could sit as close to her as the pliability of our skin could manage. Kisses warmed. Arms hugging. Nibbles all over non-combustible properties.

My right hand caressed our breast in common. She reached over and held me tighter to the pink. I pray it is not only liquor responding. She kissed my fingers, didn't budge when I took her thrust for a little circle. She pushed it at me for more. In a flash it was back in the bra. That was ok, I mean not really ok with me, right to go with what I hoped for next Wednesday or Sunday.

"Denya, I should look at the healing where the strap dug in. I promise no "hanky, panky". Would you like me to check?"

"Of course, that's very caring of you. You don't have to prove your celibacy every step of the way. "Hanky panky" is an interesting idiom. Could you demonstrate?"

"I will do a 'movie trailer' of that in a minute. That's a short advertisement before a movie. Could you get some antibiotic crème and a big Band-Aid?"

Re-arranged my attacker while she was gone. When she got back, I concentrated on crème depth and band aid angle. Bringing my hands both from behind her, I joined them at midriff and gave a good bounce to the breasts.

"That would be one variance of 'hanky panky."

"I'm not drunk as you might think. And Lance, you are not the first man of my life. I see what you are trying to do to hide yourself. I know you are restraining yourself. That's the right thing for this early relationship. I'm not ignorant of the urges. If we continue, I promise I won't be shy asking to share your masculinity."

CHAPTER FIVE

Costa Brava

No relief and additional tension came from watching her perform. Relief approached with summer vacation. In Spain most businesses close in August. Denya does no lessons nor acts. I promise I will have her, resort or not. I was a water guy and she would be a water girl. I gave her a red Scuba II training book to concentrate on. I e-mailed the resort letting them know I would be delayed on the candidate in Madrid.

We arrived at the sea hotel I had booked and still hadn't been "skin diving". We had a king bed and we slept together. In that potentially auspicious setting with suggestive ceiling décor, I only got as far as lightly caressing her precipice. After dating so long, second base was not appropriate. No "diving?" I was beginning to worry that in spite of the "I love you", she may love girls, not boys.

She was able to scuba in limited areas. Second day in a wetsuit we were scuba buddies. We dove in water up to 30 feet. Reef life was rich. Forty yards off shore, under the water, was a huge wall. It dropped down to 60 feet. The wall had some lobsters and even a Moray Eel. How she handled this could be a game-changer. Solid curricula from the resort point of view.

She looked down. I was out in the deep near the surface. Her forward momentum and light current carried her away from the wall. I saw flailing of arms. She had a B.C. set carefully by me. The current had spooked her. She was in no danger. She had doubts. Finns pounding, I arrived to take her arm in less than fifteen seconds. She made a try to climb on me to get to the surface. I had seen those eyes before. Using my lifesaving cross-chest carry I turned her away from me. Though she may try to flail, she couldn't get me. I chanced turning her back to me to see her eyes. I was much heavier and even adrenalin would not put me in danger. She came around and saw me and I could see some spark. Panic gone she got it and there was an explosion of air as she laughed into her regulator. She was relaxed again.

We kept our hands together and created a four-pointed star. Rolling out, I came up behind her and pulled her wetsuit covered booty firmly into my middle. I reached up and squeezed before my balance caused me to fall away. I took my regulator out, put my mask in a locatable place on my tank, reversed position under her gap, and unsnapped her tab. I flipped her tab up out of the way. Warm tongue, no obstruction, quick preview, no rejection. A shiver.

CHAPTER SIX

Home Plate

I had run out of patience for my masculinity. Running out of breath, I put her together again. Regulator in, mask on, there was heavy air use in both tanks. There was no way she could do this for me. Holding her breath wouldn't last the tease. What I could see in her mask approached a smile.

Showering together, both nude, was a non-starter. Celibate, except for second base, for over two months now, made me randy as a two-pecker Billy-goat. There is no way I wouldn't bend her over and take her hanging onto the shower control.

As far as I was emotionally concerned, tonight was now or never for a job offer as well as my heart. I had come to the door of her apartment in Madrid three times with intentions of breaking if off. Each time she opened the door, she was so gorgeous, I swallowed it and with a voluptuous kiss, settled for second base. This complicated my hormonal system incurably.

She showered, me in a room where I couldn't see her. I heard the shower stop and went in. I showered, even dried my hair. With a towel I walked into the bedroom.

She was under a sheet on the bed. Her breasts were breathing, breaking the surface. On her side, the swell of hips begging for a baby. She rolled to her back, hair still damp, pushed the sheet off, and waited a beat while I viewed. She reached both arms up beckoning me, throwing the towel. I went over and held myself over her. She reached over, lined me up, and pulled me down. I collapsed; wand buried.

"Lance, darling. I was so wrong. Please take me, immediately. Let it be part of my apology. Quickly, don't endure. Don't resist. Keep Yes!"

She moaned a happy recipient of my warmth. She rolled to her side, breasts brushing my chest.

"Lance there is more."

I told my mother about our closeness, and she cried, "No, no don't lose your heart to a foreigner. He will use you and go back to his country and forget you. It has happened thousands of times, millions of times. Don't make such a mistake!"

"My body had been telling me for a month that I should succumb. When I thought of you, heard your name, or your voice, I was damp. When you playfully, led us through underwater romance, it was clear. When you sought out my heat under water and teased it, it was an electric torch. I surrendered. I would risk my happiness on you in spite of my mother."

CHAPTER SEVEN

No Easy Letdown

Hesitatingly I responded, "I know the time will soon come when I must return to my scuba dream. I will go. I was here so long because I accidently fell in love. I realize I can't uproot you from your blazing career. I would never. Could never. You know you can't give up such a stunning life to be a scuba diver in a jungle. I was foolish to even dream such an impossible thing. No more now. Let's love again, it's your turn."

We loved fully over and over in a hotel down in Barcelona. Flamenco: love: monuments: love: Day cruise in Mediterranean cabin: love. It's a big city, love, enough for a lifetime. I had to leave a dear one for a career one.

We returned. Tomorrow would be our last day in the Costa Brava. Prepared, it was still heart-wrenching. I was so sorry I had made her mother right. I would never label this loss of an ideal scuba partner a waste of recruiting time. I would live the rest of my life with her memory every night. One slower sweet loving tonight. All night.

CHAPTER EIGHT

Candidate Two: Madeline, Elementry Teacher, Germany

Greg had Cheryl; in Germany I was pretty much alone. My German was only for dinner and finding a museum. If she doesn't speak English, I am a boring date. There were other emergency options. Although they were dazzling and well endowed, I didn't like the idea of paying. I had been successful in university without. Patiently, but determinedly, I was searching. The Expat bar where we got Cheryl the job was basically all English, perhaps a few bilinguals.

I continued searching for a European for the resort, possibly an American woman with some foreign language plus European ties.

As flashing eyes can do, I was struck and didn't mention the resort until our second 'after-love' bubble. It was a party dress, like a teacher half-heartedly dressing for a party. It was a third-grade teacher at the base American School. Once you raised your focus, you forget any kind of dress. The eyes direct you, influence you. I could imagine how happy third grade boys and girls would be seeing those at 8 a.m. each morning. They would do anything for her. I WOULD do anything for her. I would do some serious 'any-things' for her. I had to find a conservative line that would appeal to a conservative teacher.

A casual bar-meeting, and someone I didn't know introduced her to me. No hit-line required. Maddy and Lance. We shared who and from where. No dreaming about where we might go.

Early, we established our single status.

In the depth of German winter in February, the holiday of Fasching created a cultural rebellion. People dressed as in an American Halloween. Kids were allowed early evenings. Later evenings it was trick or drink for the adults. Winters are only a mild cold as compared to a mid-west February. Many women had mini-costumes of most transparent allure. They diminished enticingly when the activities moved indoors. This is a buxom crowd. The new beige, was pink.

I invited Maddy, wearing something under a warm cape and me professional as a pirate. I soon learned "Maddy" would be inappropriate for this woman. We started down to the party center, Sachsenhausen, in Frankfurt. It was mobbed, colors like fireworks at night. Sachsenhausen in a hollow in a wind break. The beer had been flowing, pink cheeks on all sides. Many of those pink cheeks were on women, often other pinkies. There is no conservative reveler on Fasching in Germany, even a teacher. Topless was all around outside, more intense inside bars where accoutrements didn't quickly freeze.

My gaze was traveling joyously from beauty to beauty. Maddy had experienced Fasching. She got caught up in being part of another culture, especially in a raucous celebration. Her eyes tried to command mine. I was hardly noticing her. With a high growl and a flurry, she threw off the cape. She will not be upstaged in the eyes of her date, ever, or never again! What was left was the lead female singer in Cabaret, black net garters, only make-up anywhere else, Maddy no more. A voluptuous 'Madeline', worth every syllable of her name. My eyes were hers to command.

Whatever conservatism haunted me dissipated. We whirled and kissed in all corners of the bar. The passion burst and my knees were weak. The "crush" leaped. Her eyes were glazed. As much mauling as one could do appropriately was our mission. Nothing maintained her breasts. My gaze had new focus. I had to rearrange appendages. She saw and half-heartedly tried to help. Brazen! With a constant supply of beer, we sang the traditional folklore songs with hearty loud ein svei gesufa.

The party went late and Madeline showed her true colors matching me with every dance and drink. As the crowds thinned, we caught a tram. More raucous partying. We agreed that going to my house at that hour, with bleary-eyed German driving going on, would be much safer than her place on the base. Both our eyes showed that the driving or distance was hardly the point. Cape on, we got off at the nearest stop. We hurried through the cold, damp and up to the first floor of my apartment.

We walked through the door. Turning back, the cape was waved to meld us together and the kiss passion-laced crushed us close.

I removed the cape and most of my pirate-ship. We shared the disrobing and she was again up against the door booties in my hands. The kiss crashed and control was hers. She slid right down.

We had both been alone a long time. We were crushed, teased, and implanted over and over until sunrise. The curtains were closed and we slept the sleep of the loved. This pirate had had his timbers shivered.

Sunday beckoned and I learned her intense creativity. Way above third grade! We brought our "wild" out of boundaries beyond fire. Warm holding; lovingly caressing bookended our starts. I made sure she had as many "turns" as I. Without exception.

I spent the next month walking on air, running to the base to bring her back to my place. Schedules permitted trysts on Wednesday evenings and weekends, all weekend. The melted comfort of post-firing pillow talk took us far into dreaming. I explained about my passion for the scuba operation.

Having been in Germany years more than I, she took me to the castles on the Rhine and the Hofbrau House in Munich. We frequently went to small Dorfs within a day's drive for a new beer and new beds. A few sofas.

My next trip to Central America was scheduled after her school finished for the summer. My lights blinked on and I realized I was learning to know the perfect partner for the scuba resort. She didn't scuba. As instructor I could quickly train her. A teacher would already be caring for divers, a bonus for me, beautiful.

A full summer of scuba clubs; I invited and she agreed. School person she was, she checked the Kama Sutra from the library for the summer. Some raised eyebrows, but they had been at Fasching. Her family would come to Frankfurt for a week in May; going on to other European adventures. We went southwest. Greg and I had been doing extremely well with salaries and royalties; Cheryl couldn't keep up with demand. I could easily provide the ticket. She hadn't even been as far south as Florida.

I sensed some discomfort in Madeline after she saw me dealing with most airline communication in Spanish in Miami. Spanish was mine, only German was hers.

In seven hours of jet lag, we learned our layover in Miami, scheduled to be two hours, due to someone's screw-up would be four hours. Embarrassed, since I had hoped to show her the good-times she had shown me in Germany, I headed for the bar. I had rerouted the luggage to LANSA air from TACA. She relaxed somewhat after a tall one, and I told her the joke about the airline names on these southern routes. Lansa, Lineas Aereas Nationales South America was translated to "Lost and Never Seen Again." The bigger one going into Cosa Rica was TACA, "Take a Coffin long." I need to keep my loving skills shipshape; my joke telling is poor.

We were well-oiled but irritable at the short separation between rows of seats and three on each side. It was only two hours to San Pedro Sula. We steeled ourselves to tough it out. The atmosphere was not warm. I felt uncomfortable thinking about what she was feeling. No food beyond peanuts and pay for all drinks including water didn't help matters. We still had two additional flights to get to the island.

In SPS, we had another one-hour delay. The plane to Cuenca on the North Coast was a DC-5, a plane first built for WWII. Not beautiful, it was one of the most durable and secure planes ever built. We're now nine hours into jet lag and she is not impressed. Reluctantly she journeyed on.

In small Cuenca, we exited our plane and walked over to the final. It was a four-passenger including the pilot. I could sense a "fight or flight' emotion but she delicately climbed up into the back seat with our suit cases. Her face was stone, no emotion, like she had no hope of survival.

When the plane began to touch down on the gravel landing strip for Guanaja, she leaped and buried herself in my arms, shuddering, until it stopped. She flew out, a flash, kissing the ground. Classical, of course, but I was hoping she would be working at my resort.

I got the luggage and held her for a long time. Nothing said. Eventually, Trey in one of the support boats arrived to take us to the resort. She was not fearful of boats but wasn't smiling.

Walking up to my air-conditioned cabana, she got two mosquito bites. I hurried her into the cabana and applied repellant. Seeing the shower, she was out of her clothes and into my dream. She was humming a quiet intense tone of stress even after being there twenty minutes. I was waiting to hold her. She went directly to the bed, covered herself, put some repellent on her face, arms and neck and fell asleep.

She slept all the way through until the next morning at 10:00 a.m. I had a light dinner and a heavy rum drink and crawled in and slept next to her. She started twice in the night, disoriented; lost. I was right there and rocked her back asleep.

I was right there in the morning, too. Having forgotten where she was and what she had gone through, and that I was right tight there, I got a smile and a crusher kiss. Unfortunately, things went only slightly uphill from there and shockingly downhill thereafter.

I slipped out of my cabana and returned with some coffee for her, an island fruit and a home-made roll. She was still lying down but raised up and took the food with another smile. I talked a little and she vaguely listened. She agreed to learn to snorkel and see some underwater wild life and fauna. She got up, full frontal and took another shower. When she came back, I was waiting with the repellant to cover her. Finished, I had repellant all over me.

In happier pre-flight times, she had packed some very short shorts and a T-shirt which I am sure she brought for me. No bra. Torture, only temporary, I hoped.

We walked down to the dock where both dive boats were gone to reefs north-east of the Island. I got her snorkel, mask and fins and we headed east through soft white sand. The pier was long and wide, painted white in a "T" shape, a place for both ramp-tail boats and the security to conveniently dock. There was another retired airport boat with its nose attached to an old gnarly coconut tree.

By the time we got the 60 meters to the snorkel reef, we were both soaked and she had won the wet blouse contest. We arrived at a portion of reef which had been formed long ago. A coral head had been broken off a wall by a monster storm. The wave action had been immense that rather than the length of broken reef falling to the bottom, it had been carried within forty meters of the shore. The rock was now thirty meters long by three meters wide in four meters of water. Much of the original coral remained with significant amounts of new coral and plant life. The wall was still there, 150 meters out. A perfect spot for a new snorkel experience. My eyes, of course were not as much on the coral as on the wet t-shirt snorkeler. Diving buddies must stay near each other. We fondled around a half hour surfacing for air and some maritime information from me.

Following, I came around behind her as she reached into a hole in the wall. I lunged, but too late. A wild stirring in the water with sand filling the water around me, an eel burst out of the hole, mouth open! Given any escape route, eels don't mess with creatures 20 times as big as them. Frightened and disoriented, it coursed around, grazed her calf, slimy rough skin, and shot off into the distance. She shot up out of the water screaming. I was right there, used my life saver approaches and got her into shallow water. The fright on her face was palpable. I held her and tried to talk her down.

She said, "Lance, I've got to go back. Out of the water now". She didn't use the snorkel again. She was frightened and I was heart-broken. One of my greatest joys in life and at the moment she hated it.

The warm sand by the pier was creature-free if you didn't look too deep. Nothing to snorkel for. The water was still fresh. In later summer, it was too warm and you couldn't wait to get to the thermal clime. Especially if you were in a wet suit. We jumped in and out and her face became friendly. Cautiously friendly. Then sunburned. I ran to the kitchen and got the sun cream SPF 50 to save her that pain. I should have put it on with the mosquito repellant but I was 100% distracted. Her face was a bit red, her back and legs golden tan. Delicious. We rolled around, additional supplicating caresses of cream from me, and eventually the dive boats came back. Thirty on each boat. She watched as I went and helped my captains disrobe the divers of tanks, B.C.s, fins and weight belts.

Within thirty minutes of the boat's arrival, happy hour started in the bar and restaurant. I got her there early to try to wash away her difficult day. She had a few, didn't open up to any of the divers to chat. We had dinner and went down to the dock to watch the moon guand stars. Another quiet time. It was stunningly romantic and we kissed a few times. She was again in a tight t-shirt with no bra. I guess she didn't bring any.

With the sun gone and the tiki torches showing the way to the cabanas, she said, "I'm sweating. Your cabana has an air conditioner, right? This humidity is killing me."

We walked up with sweat running down her back and front.

She was huffing when we arrived. She stripped and headed straight for a cool shower. As she was finishing, I went in to rinse the salt off. We passed, both naked, didn't grope. We dried and she went to the bed first. When I came, she was welcoming, but mild. We hugged a while as I was debating which whirlwind position, I could use to charm her tonight. She turned to me leading with the buxom girl's firm on my chest. With eyes and no words, she made it clear she needed me emotionally and forcefully physically, but not fast. Slow and sinuous.

Slowly, I could take her for a long ride. I did and burst. She cooed, "Your warmth!" I smoothly slid down where I could return the favor. The demand for seeding after near death may be true.

"Lance, oh god, I needed that to be sure I am alive."

We laid once again on our backs in those open vulnerable moments. I had nothing to say, but felt a hurt in the touches. She finally took a deep breath and said, "Lance, I've got to go. Not tonight of course, but get me the small torture plane as early as possible in the morning before the wind comes up. I know you love this life and Germany is just a stop on your way. I respect your skills and ability to help these people have wonderful experiences. The heat, the humidity, mosquitos, sand fleas, sunburn, fear of what I don't know, I can't force myself to tolerate even in exchange for the deep love you offer. Hold me tonight, please come with me to San Pedro Sula, then let me go. Perhaps we can communicate by skype or when you get back to Germany."

I agreed to her wishes; didn't sleep a wink. I knew I would never be able to anticipate every anomaly of an ever-changing reef. She didn't have any nightmares that I noticed. I gently moved her off to San Pedro. I couldn't force her to stay for more fear. Seeing her, I would be destroyed, too. Another potential quality partner lost.

We skyped a couple of times. I returned to Germany in October. For a while I hung out with Greg and his wife. I stayed away from the base near Frankfurt. I did one platonic call to confirm I was back in Germany. My insides still hurt from the loss. I knew who I was and what I dreamed. I hoped there would be another out there who would enjoy joining me in the same dream.

away from the base near Frankfurt. I did one platonic call to confirm I was back in Germany. My insides still hurt from the loss. I knew who I was and what I dreamed. I hoped there would be another out there who would enjoy joining me in the same dream.

CHAPTER NINE

Futures

In the fawning pride of Greg, I was introduced to the new Mercedes executives on rotation. We had continually been forwarding ideas with my designs. Nothing was mentioned about my office on Guanaja.

We were all studying some form of business or engineering, some land based, me marine based, and Roberto Sea Agriculture. We drank beer, played hoops and dreamed together. Roberto would vacate his suite occasionally when Greg or I were "entertaining." Roberto and I had pretty solid plans. With Greg's didactic mind, he could find work anywhere. I dreamed of owning a scuba-based resort in the Caribbean and with the share of the patent could do it without parental support. With Roberto's contacts, I was soon building the cabanas, buying a second ramp boat, looking into marketing not only in the U.S. but in Europe. I went to Spain a month after Roberto. We never met again until some years later back in Guanaja.

Roberto, with good support from his family had his eye on a shrimp farm. Luckily the U.S. Senator from the south on the Cartels "Lempira payroll" wasn't aware of another bribe opportunity. The farm was adjacent to the big island pertaining to Honduras. His father struggling to operate in an ethical manner in a government inundated with drug cartel money, had been there long enough to survive. He and Roberto were both studying the options. His Dad agreed to a year's trip through Europe before developing the farm.

Roberto was studying off and on, Castilian, at the Official School of Language in north Madrid. He spoke Spanish and English growing up. He only needed to tone his listening skills and pronounce the "theta" style use of the for z. We spoke often about the development of the resort where he had actively participated. He knew of the expansion requiring an additional woman partner and European marketing. He would, of course, support the search, but at the moment, had no idea I was attending Zarzuelas in Madrid, a few kilometers away.

It would be a year and a half later before he would recount this experience and that of a woman potential candidate he had met in Callao. It was a saga in itself.

CHAPTER TEN

Melissa: Marketing Model
Recruiting German Marketing Contract

There were several local men available to captain the ramp boats and cook and tend bar. Some dive clubs included women members and we didn't have one. I had tried and lost several in Spain due to the place they were in their careers, or their fear of underwater creatures. I think some may have been frivolous with the applications. The position would be a full partnership but hadn't drawn a mature candidate. I was still trying but now needed to concentrate on increased marketing. We also needed to extend our marketing specifically to Europe from where we had had three walk-in clubs. Our website and brochures were attracting U.S. divers, but Western Europe needed development.

In Spain, I had some joyous extended recruiting meetings for the partnership, but no serious nor appropriate candidate. I booked a flight from Barajas up to Munich. Greg and Cheryl were on vacation. I advertised both jobs, but got no sensible candidate for the partnership. The modeling contract was a whole different experience, successful this time.

There were some modeling agencies, bilingual groups on the Marienstrasse near the famous Lowenbrau Brewery. Booked in at the Lands Berger Hotel the night before, I walked over to the Marienstrasse for breakfast among many, many Germans and tourists. Parked on the sides of the Marienstrasse were scores of cars to be sold second-hand. Set back from this street were several huge buildings holding scores of offices and hundreds of apartments. The bottom two or three floors held major department stores. Kaufhof, C&A, Bauhaus to name three. Between those buildings and the cars were open air restaurants. If it were not raining, chairs were full. It was cold but sunny.

In front of the C&A store were several theater Kleig instruments. Off. I ordered a hot chocolate, large, and sat toward the back of the café near the cars. Everybody is looking around at everybody continuing chatting or starting new chats. The German, too difficult for me.

The Kleigs came on bathing the door and the front of the store in soft light. A photographer and assistants scurried out. Tripods set up and video placed. Some gay looking guys came out holding some fluffy material. Wrapped in that material was a female form. It was a little far from me to see. The boys unwrapped the female who had her hair up in some sophisticated style. No-one would see the face if that stayed where it was. Dammed if I didn't know her. No one would be looking at the face because the girl was nude except for her stilettos. She struck various poses; the photo assistant guided her and turned her according to what the photographer shouted. I thought I must have lost my lucidity.

She swayed over to the Platinum red Mercedes. She caressed it lovingly. It was shocking. She mounted the hood holding the Mercedes symbol between her knees. The movement of mounting exposed her thighs to the depths. A few men were shifting in their seats. She used her thighs to stroke other parts of the hood. The dismount was calculated to take the swell behind the male zippers to maximum. She lounged her way to the left car-side door, opened it, and bent forward inside to adjust something. Pre-meditated booty view! Striking. Three couples went hurriedly into the building. 'Thrust' would be the word. They were the foreign tourists. Most of the German men and women alike never looked up except to smirk at the tourists in their dishabille.

She adjusted for maximum time of male survival. She got

in, having a little trouble with her stilettos, which caused her legs to go completely open. She smiled and closed them slowly. Obviously programmed. Closed the door. Photographer came and took a photo down into the car from above the door. Titties turning the wheel. She opened the door, put her legs out first. Fields of thighs. Any tourist with a camera was in action. The photographer growled about copyright and put an end to that. She strode again to the fender of the car and bent over to give a hug. Leaving the booty shaking, she gave a final twerk of disrespect and headed again to the hood of the car. She laid across the front hood, looked up and met my eyes. Frozen smile. Moved on.

She got off now looking disgusted, threw a rude twerk, and headed for the muscled gay guys with her wrap.

I sat there breathless. I wanted to do something. I sat there frozen. I decided to wait and see what might happen if she emerged from that C&A door. I knew she was a model, perfect for a white sand beach scuba resort.

It wasn't long, and Melissa, now I remembered, came out of the door with a warm-up suit. Without a hesitation she headed toward my row, my seat. She took me by the hand, not much more passionate than a greeting at a funeral. "I knew from your brochure picture you were here. I saw you stand up when I came out. Walk with me. Please don't touch me now. I'll explain later. We need to leave this place now; it has to do with my advertising contract. Don't hold my hand. Try to let on this is a business meeting. Please be patient and all will be well."

I shut up. We sat at a table, she on the other side. I stumbled on what to say in a business meeting. She saw my discomfort and gave me leading subjects and lines I could use to generate a fake play of discussion. She said, "Ok that's enough."

"Now, Lance, walk with me very demurely, not too close, no touching, like I was your sister. Here's our situation. If I were free, I would have your hands and fingers caressing me all over. You were magic in Spain, now, please don't react. You will have a mountain of chances later. Listen! The bottom line of my contract here is to sell Mercedes automobiles. I am a central part of this advertising campaign. I know shit about any automobile, what I am actually selling is myself. It's more complicated than that.

If you ever had a psychology class in your college preparation, you may be able to follow this. In the last 20 minutes, I have "fucked" the Mercedes for all the heterosexual men in this audience. In their mind, and for some hours later, they will unconsciously feel that I will be part of the purchase price. The longer that lasts, or re-occurs, the higher the number of sales.

In the meantime, they saw me nude, but also recognized me when I left the building. They will all be asking themselves how they can get into my pants. I have created a bubble of existence for them. If the bubble stays in existence, chance of sales going up is high. If I did well enough, and I did, that attitude will remain in their sub-conscious and they will have an affinity to that shape of car. If they see me in any level of passionate relationship with you, the bubble will burst and sales may be affected.

Now, this is not a forever binding document. I have done my job. Their lust has been enhanced. Many are still under the trance that I will be in the car. Mercedes paid half of my fee in advance. I will go and collect the remainder tomorrow.

"Lance, what hotel are you in?"

"I'm in the Munich Lands Berger hotel, three blocks from here, up that way."

"Lance, go to your registration desk, get your key and inform them your wife will be coming soon and please give her a second key. I will be Mrs. Starr, for a while. Or, we'll see."

A quiet knock at the door, and all the tall parts of her were intensely up against me. "Lance, please settle me first. Later, it's your turn."

Cheryl had introduced me to Melissa in one of her match-maker phases when I came alone to Germany from Guanaja. While we did date for a while, I did know she was a model, but not this much of a model. I wasn't looking for a woman partner for the resort at that time. I knew she was very connected in Europe and Los Angeles. Although my resort was doing well, even a partnership would not be in her league. She left for some shoot, up in Sweden and I hadn't even communicated with her again.

A surprised but stunningly all-passion kiss; both to our knees.

"Lance, please let me stop. I have been dreaming of feeling exactly this expansion for five months. I held little hope of seeing you again unless I decided to try scuba. Relax, let me glow in your desire."

I was on fire. This was the finest woman a man could imagine, much less capture. After five months, I now realized I had been the last guy.

"Lance, I'm starting. Move the hoody away, up above."

"Before words", I responded.

"Oh, heaven. Without asking, you remember. I'm in love with every part of you. I must explode! Get out of the way at your peril."

There was no hesitation here. We had in a very few words re-kindled a now continuing relationship. She had left her rational world behind for the enthralling rush of the great release. Some women call it the "little death". They are disillusioned. It is the celebration of human heaven on earth.

She has said and now proven again her vulnerability to me. It is such an honor and privilege. Both know there is little possibility of survival across two continents with meetings only time and again.

We grasp and take what we can. This is the woman I desire

to share in magnificent movement. It is the sound of the mature woman who paints my hearing. She starts with the murmur of breathlessness, breaks into intense moans, and collapses.

I celebrate, moving her into our post-loving bubble.

"Melissa, maybe we should take a nap or settle in for the night. You must be tired pretending all that trick stuff for Mercedes."

"Lance, you can be shallow. You took me to energy depletion forty times the energy used as the silly Mercedes model."

I did my best to kiss her passion, love her neck, and caress her breasts.

"Lance, enough. I am not begging for foreplay after five months."

Tomorrow became the afternoon and I had to explore if we could contract her for the Starr Scuba Resort. I expected to receive no special discounts, her standard and travel pay scale. We had little time for champagne but made a date in Guanaja for two weeks later on a Sunday. I gave her the shooting schedule pending acceptable weather. She marked it up with several extended periods of re-charge time. I smiled. She was used to charging in 220volts. Grab what you can, prepare to weather a broken heart.

CHAPTER ELEVEN

CANDIDATE 4: MS Phillips

She was in 8th grade, a beauty with a rack. I didn't know what a rack was because I was only in 5th grade. I had seen a few naked classmates but they didn't have racks. I did know what a beauty was. She lived on the other side of the lake, like a distance that could never be navigated. I saw her only in our little K-8 elementary school.

If you are in 5th grade and the girl is in 8th, she won't even acknowledge your existence. You are a lower creature. She would be embarrassed among her friends if she even talked to you. I, in turn, in my emotional force field, was sick for her.

One valentine's day, I purchased a big red heart of chocolates. I went to give it to her at recess. She pushed them back at me in a nasty way and said she didn't want them. I was crushed; distraught.

My first really hurtful heart break. Her family moved away at the end of that year. I never saw her in high school. I never thought I would see her again. I never forgot her.

A few decades later, owner of a Scuba resort in the Bay Islands, I spent some of the winter in the Midwest, nostalgic. This time the trip was tax deductible, as a critical position was open at the resort. I spent most of the time east near the large metropolitan city of Milwaukee with many performance venues.

This weekend, aficionado of live theater, I drove four hours west. I was in Dubuque on the Mississippi attending a presentation of "Pump Boys and Dinettes". A moderately funny show not riveting. I wasn't constantly focused on the stage. My eyes wandered around the audience. Not thinking of her recently, I saw a woman, older of course, with a familiar profile. Her profile had been stunning as I remembered. I didn't take this seriously. I did think of her. It had been many years. I wasn't sure I would even recognize her. I didn't live in Dubuque; in fact, I lived 4 hours away near my home town where I had loved her from afar and lost her.

When she had moved away from grade school, I didn't know where she had gone. I refocused on the show and forgot about the errant thoughts.

I hadn't seen this show and loved musicals. I had driven over, rented a hotel for the night and went.

Long with two intermissions. I patronized the "in-theater" concessions when their profits go the civic theater.

I turned away from the bar, which forced my view towards the lady's room. Always embarrassed by this, I moved to turn away quickly. In the spin, my eyes were arrested. Coming out of the room was, or was it, my Ms. Phillips. Her name was Patty I remembered. I wasn't confident enough to move to her. I couldn't keep my eyes away. I'm a big guy and don't think she missed me. She didn't speak. I completed my spin and she went in to the theater. I went back to my seat for the next act. I didn't concentrate much on the play. I frequently glanced her way to try to be sure I was right. I think she caught some of the glances. I wasn't sure.

The second act ended. Another intermission. I am now certain it was her. I had had some experiences along the way and developed my self-confidence. I had missed some opportunities by being shy. I was not going to miss another by being afraid to approach her. "Excuse me. My name is Lance Starr. I apologize if I am making a mistake here, my memory tells me you are Patty Phillips. We were in elementary school together."

"Yes, Lance, I thought it was you. You haven't changed much

in lots of years. Your face has stayed rugged and thin. I'm actually Patty Burns now. My husband passed away five years ago and I haven't seen a need to change it."

She was about '5"10' with long brown hair. I could tell it was lightly colored. The "rack" was still uplifting. The lines in her face expressed a long-time life of caring. Sometimes sadness. Her face had high, flat planes with a nose of character. Strong chin led to a model's long, supple neck. Her lips could express any emotion; her eyes, flashing, said much more.

"Patty, the show is going to begin soon. We need to go back. I have some feelings I would regret if I didn't share with you. Could we get together tonight or tomorrow and catch up?"

"I'm free. We could also sit together for the third act. There is a seat open next to me."

"Great, we can make other plans."

After the show, late, we made a date for the next day. There was a replica of a 1950's diner a stone's throw from the theater. She lived in Dubuque, it was walking from her house. We met for an early dinner at 5 p.m.

"Patty, when you knew me, probably not well, in fifth grade, I was awkward in my speech. Star struck! From my side, I was fiercely into you, too shy to say. I'm better now. I'll start before I lose my nerve. We have years to catch up on".

I went on about my single life traveling and living in nine different countries. Her non-verbal reactions were what I could hope they would be.

"Lance, after we moved, I ended up in Lancaster High School. After living in the Milwaukee area, this was pure farm society. There was little to do and the boys knew they were going back to the farm. They had little motivation to do school work. I knew I could never settle for the life they would give.

I did well, however, in high school and won a half scholarship at Northwestern. Although Mom tried to keep me nearby, I bolted to NU and knew soon I would be happy. I would be a sorority girl. This opened up a sumptuous social life and I would never go home again except to visit. A girl with some taste of life, I left the U alone to take a job as an accountant here in Dubuque. The company 3M had a branch here and I was there at the right time and right place. Still not a Milwaukee, Dubuque had a night life and many cultural offerings.

I soon learned that a bachelor's degree from university didn't prepare one well enough for accounting in the real world. The recruiter had seen this before, He set me up with an older more experienced auditor. In short, this Glen guided me through the bumps and grinds of accountancy in that setting. He marched me directly up the aisle to the preacher and we were married. It was maybe not that direct. We did practice some of the lighter side of marriage before we tied the knot. Not for long though. We knew what we wanted and had recognized it quickly.

She went on to note she had gotten her masters and there was a married daughter living with her son-in-law in Holland. Sometimes they scheduled visits with holidays.

Our third time together, things got more intimate. We had started dinner later. We left soon. The moon was out. At the doorstep, I moved in for the hoped kiss. It was there. It was not one of those air kisses you see in Europe and places further east. I had finally kissed my 5th grade flame. Like a teenager, I skipped to the hotel.

I had to be out of town the next day and she had an audit she could schedule. We didn't see each other that night. The following day we headed for the diner again and talked personally. We were venturing out to what we might agree on in the world; on what we might not agree. This was an awakening of what we shared in common. The exception, of course, was watching the Green Bay Packers football.

Her late husband, Glen, although originally from Illinois was a Packer fan and clearly had little respect for the Chicago Bears. That's how his name came in to our discussion. She also commented our sleeping alone the previous night without seeing each other had been notably "lonely".

She offered this comment of feeling about the loneliness. I have always had to be the one to risk sharing such feelings. It made me nervous every time. What joy and difference to have it come from her first. Here I got a hug in, even in the diner.

It sparked my hunger. My goal changed to a man and still beautiful woman. Our male animal nature and ego cause us theoretically to want to have a child with this beauty. Together, we see how beautiful and smart would be the offspring. My theory anyway. In reality, another child at this time in our lives would not be comfortable. My mind was wandering.

For her, the hug had very intense meaning. I could sense it physically. Then it really came out. Emotionally. We had not said much about previous relationships. Her late husband, although important, hadn't come up. Until now! Thanks to the Packers.

"Lance, we have quickly re-connected. I need to share this. It is important I do this. For me, I absolutely have to let it out."

"Patty, whatever you want, I am interested in all your thoughts."

She went on to recount that (married) part of her life. They had been together many years. She talked about their meeting in 3M and how the relationship had developed. Glen knew a beauty when he saw one and set his hat with no other acceptable option. He pursued her until she caught him. He found her every joy and involved himself in sharing. He didn't particularly love opera, she did and he quickly had season tickets to the one over in Milwaukee. It took him less than a year to capture her heart and give her an engagement ring. The rest of their time together with the exception of the daughter's adolescence growing pains was all positive.

There had been some symptoms of illness a few months before he died. What happened was not a complete surprise out of the dark. The death of one she had loved so dearly was an emotional shock and grievous heartbreak.

"Lance, we woke up one morning. We shared a couple night-tasting kisses and he quickly stood up. He had no sooner got to his feet than he collapsed. I was still sitting up on the bed and thought he may have been playing some joke. He didn't move. I called 911 and tried to do some CPR. There was some little response so I kept going until the rescue squad came. For me the response had stopped. I left him to open the door for the EMT's. They took over and transported him to the hospital. They had the siren wailing and were traveling fast. I was hopeful there was still some chance.

At the hospital he was rushed to the emergency room. Shortly later, they took him to surgery. Nobody could tell me anything one way or the other. I would rather die than have to live through such an experience again.

After the surgery, the doctor came to see me. He said it had been a massive stroke. They had cleaned the area affected. Chances were small. They moved him to intensive care where I remained immovable.

Two days later in the night, I was holding his hand and felt a small movement. I went to look in his eyes and they were active, clear. Pain strained his face.

He said, "Honey, it's so hard. Would it be alright with you if I go over"?

My breath caught as I realized what he was asking. Would I give him permission? I knew what had to be done. I told him I loved him forever, kissed him softly and said, "Go, darling, go to where you don't hurt."

The lights in his eyes faded.

We were the last ones in the diner and all staff eyes were full. I waited while she regathered her strength. I ordered us a coffee with a shot. I walked her home arms entwined and stopped for a thoughtful kiss at the door. Bodies were seeking each other with not an inch of distance. It was not the right night to seal a relationship after hearing the tearful end of another.

Lance, she said, "I feel better and probably shouldn't have waited. While a catharsis, it leaves me bushed. I need more spirit to share other things with you. I am not blind to where you, we, are heading with this relationship. I need one day to put things in perspective, the vulnerability I would be trusting to you. An unexpected fresh new start. Huge gear change, a miracle, Lance. Please come over tomorrow night."

I went home, got online and bought the remainder of the opera tickets for the present season.

I arrived at her house at 4 in the afternoon with my suitcase packed. She met me at the door with a glow. She had had her catharsis. There was no doubt. She pulled me in the door, nudged me against the back of it, thrust her body with every curve sensing me. She tipped her head back to see my eyes, paused a beat, and took me into a kiss vibrating my shoestrings.

We had a quick dinner. She hadn't been loved for a long time and was absorbing every nuance. Desert would be on the bed. All you need to know about a lover was intensified in her eyes and her touch.

"Lance, lover, let's not bide any more. Come gentle, slow and quiet. It's been so long. She opened and reached her arms up for me. Filmy legs around me. "I want you to be on top. Don't worry, I'm a big girl. You won't hurt me."

"Doze with me if you wish, she said, "you're not leaving this house or bed in the foreseeable future. Warmed up, so gentle, so quiet. I'm healing."

"The visiting doctor is not done!" Entranced, I began. What a long wait for a 5th grader's dream!"

I tend to be gentle especially with a woman not well known to me. Long awaited, she was wildly aroused. I will not be party to any modicum of pain in the sex act. Foreplay, do whatever you want. I began it her way. I heard her say: fast; moved my lips to the exterior ellipse of her flame and began the wave. She squeaked. I increased my velocity around the swelling center. Speed like the chariots in Rome. It was a teasing sensation and I knew she hungered for more. She shrieked and throwing her midriff in the air, shuddered, panting, swearing love words. She raised her midriff, held for three beats, exploded an exhalation; wild bursts into her relief. The look in her eyes I would cherish for a lifetime.

I moved next to her on the bed. She pushed every part of her body into my body somewhere, wrapped her arms around me, melted, and said, "Your turn. I was far beyond control, and with a new, long desired woman, managed only a few seconds. She started, throaty satisfaction, "stay in me. I forgot the stunning, full feeling."

We made the opera. It was not difficult to entice her back to Milwaukee. A full circle in a lifetime.

CHAPTER TWELVE

Perfect fit, but life grows limits

I was on a mission with this special gift surprise. I told her about the resort and the job. Accounting and book-keeping, her years of experience perfect. She leaned back in the couch on my arm. She thought forever."

"Lance, I am torn apart. I know what I must do, for you and for me. You have re-opened a world I thought I would never see. I doubt any other man could do the caring things you did. If I were to accept, we would have to be married to go to Central America. As sweet as your love, I couldn't do it. I was horribly comatose when Glen died. I lost all desire and yearned to go with him. I absolutely could not face that again and live on."

If things in life changed, and we could be together, I would still have to schedule times alone, nights without you, keeping myself prepared. That is a selfish requirement and I would not expect you nor anyone to live that way. To ease this heartbreak that we are both facing, let me tell you that you are welcome here for a visit anytime, continuing everything we have shared together as though we had not been apart. I will not be married and you would be free to choose what we might share together. It need not be good bye. Au revoir. A bottle of champagne required upon return.

CHAPTER THIRTEEN

CAROLINE: ON SITE, Unexpected Benefits Package

It's always at least spring in the Bay Islands. It was a warm, humid return to Guanaja. Nothing was new of which I was unaware. Either a captain or Roberto was on Skype weekly.

The groups were getting larger for the spring and I jumped back into being boat Captain to distract myself from thinking about Cassandra's legs around my waist.

Two of our diving staff had decided to pursue their non-water careers on the mainland U.S. I immediately posted the positions on-line and, in the Miami Herald, and a smaller paper in Gulfport. I also posted it on the bar on the island.

CHAPTER FOURTEEN

THE ARRIVAL OF VANNA, Candidate 7.
(Walk-in)

Divers buy a package for this resort. For a set price, the flight and transfer of them, their equipment and pretty much everything to the dock is included. I had two large compressors with air included. Odds and ends of other equipment could be had if it happened to be available. (Watches, depth gauges, etc.) Three meals per day and one drink each happy hour plus cabana rounded out the package. A firm warning was given that they take only pictures and leave only bubbles. I had a picture of a guy kicked out early having tried to unearth a sea fan. A novice would not know that when you take one of them out of the water, it smells terrible. The only other difference was prices for people wishing to extend their stay when their package ends. They could stay for a week at 10% discount, but may have to move into a cabana not reserved by a coming group. Those were a little further away from the central toilets and didn't have a private shower. The meals and drinks continue as before. I had tried a 20% discount but it hadn't increased interest that much. The probability of a person or two extending increased, if at all, with a group of twenty-five or more. That's the only lasting morsel of information I gleaned from university "Probability". Got a "C".

There was one other resort on this island on the north side. "Nude.com". I was friendly with the owner and went over occasionally to share gripes and a rum and coke. There was not a lot of cross visiting because the jungle path was painful and the other resort was "no clothing permitted". The owner was a woman, Zulinda, with rotating guys as her main squeezes. I didn't visit a lot because she was such a momentous beauty (not a stitch), I would get out of hand quickly. I stayed a few moments to share selected things about my time in Germany. Good relations were important for both of us as we used the same supplier for many of our meal preparations. Legs crossed fifteen minutes, just mine, kept things friendly.

Moving into summer, a group of thirty reserved everything we had. Both ramped dive boats were full and the security boat took two guys who had dive instructor licenses. Two of my captains also had the licenses, as did I. With the captains, I helped get everyone into tanks and B.C., s.

There were two women in the group. Both were lovely and with good muscle tone, undoubtedly from a lot of diving. One was on each boat. The difference was only the choice of swim suit. On my boat, Vanna didn't have a thong; it wasn't much more. The girl on the other boat, Donna, had a more conservative two-piece suit. The interactions between men and women didn't include anything flirty. The women were "one of the guys" and any thoughts that I might be having, weren't echoed by the men. Maybe they were sisters or had been with the guys long, now being ignored. The other difference which was notable, at least on such a demanding dive, was Vanna's handling of the equipment. Diving is an equipment intensive sport. She donned the heavy gear asking me for a boost getting the tank in place. Strengths didn't appear until the middle of the dive and thereafter.

Sensible divers never dive alone. She had a partner. They had partnered before. I was diving above and behind the group, veritable mother hen protecting my large investment. Several times she saw him slide into rocks where the air valve of the tank would drift up and trap him. The diver's response is to bang his dive knife against the tank to signal request for help. He never got his knife into striking position before she was a foot away from him easing him down and out. They didn't need any mothering. I noted it and moved ahead.

Everybody is salty and tired from the equipment effort along with losing body heat to the water. They float up on the recovery ramp and friends or the staff help them shed their equipment starting with the weight belt. Vanna came to the ramp, thrust her body forward, rose to her feet unassisted and moved into the tank storage area. Like a flash she was out of her weight belt and tank and other gear heading back to help friends on the ramp. I could do that, a glance at my shoulders would make it obvious why. She wasn't rippling muscles. Only two deep breaths told of any effort. If you weren't watching this, you would miss it. I noted it and walked on. She looked up at me and we shared a glance a couple of beats longer than typical.

The next two days I went in the small boat with the licensed guys. I didn't dive; maintained the location of the boat in the current. Frankly, it is painful getting over the side of this boat to get back in. I prefer the ramp boat.

Happy hour, first drink free, happens as soon as people shower the salt off and dry up. Several mixed drinks or beers is not recommended. Alcohol and diving can be dangerous. The mildest repercussion is too many beers. You drink it at one atmosphere. Tomorrow, it will be in your digestive track at two or three atmospheres. Not fun.

We met each other's glance a few times over drinks. When we moved to the buffet, she was sitting at my left. We did shallow talk and she asked about any irregularities of the reef. I knew them very well. The fact that she knew enough to ask the question was added to my notes. Tempted, I didn't walk her back to her bungalow.

The week went on. She dived morning and afternoon. She did the Wednesday night dive, as well. She was clearly strong in condition as well as strength. On one occasion I was her buddy. We didn't always focus on the reef; occasional minor invasions of the other's space were mildly suggestive, but platonic.

On Friday, the day before they would leave, she came and asked about the conditions of extending her stay. The conversation was particularly warm. After drinks and dinner, I went up on the balcony above the bar to finish my drink and catch a few stars. No moon tonight. She shadowed a little later and sat next to me nursing her Southern Comfort Old Fashioned. We discussed some other diving she had seen and some, in the Caribbean, that she hadn't. We finished the conversation, sharing similar vibes. She leaned over and said she definitely wanted to extend her stay, gave me a peck on the cheek and headed off to the cabana.

CHAPTER FIFTEEN

Vanna Becomes Viable

I registered her stay the next morning and sent her out with a Captain in the small boat. She had taken a double tank and would spend some time at deeper levels. The captain would be in the water not going that deep. She would have to decompress at 10-15 feet and he would exert absolute control over that.

The dive went without incident and she was hungry for lunch. Only the staff would be there until the next weekend Food was aplenty. I ate lightly; sipped on a rum and coke. It was early afternoon and I would be in no trouble if I dove the next day. I didn't plan to. She floated away into the trees and I guessed she was feeling the time at 100 feet, and would take a nap. I moved back to my A/C., read my kindle and dozed. I got up before four o'clock to be sure I would be able to sleep that night. A day without the exercise of a dive, I decided to walk the beach.

She wasn't as tired as I guessed. She was toning the tan and making a momentous sand castle. I went over and sat in the sand. I added a wall to the castle gleaning a smile. I asked about the deep foray and said there was not much down that deep. She agreed and said she did see a huge grouper in a cave. The second it sensed me, it flashed and was nowhere to be seen.

I went over to wipe clean the tanks and B.C.s. As I rose, she did too and stepped toward me, asking if I would dive with her tomorrow. Well, she was paying the full price, she should get whomever she wanted as a dive buddy. There was a little more in the request about having me rather than another Captain. I agreed, glad I hadn't drunk a beer.

I walked over to the ramp boat and stepped aboard to clean the tanks. The boat swayed surprising me as she stepped nimbly aboard. Nothing was said but she watched what I was doing and mirrored it. It was my least favorite task and I had to do two boats, 32 tanks, weight belts, B. C's regulators, knives, and spray half as many wetsuits. I appreciated the help. As noted earlier, she needed no help in man-handling any of the heavy equipment, including her double tanks.

After moving to the second boat, conversation continued. We talked about her experience and I learned what I had here. She was a female version of me as per experience. Large group experience was my advantage to the moment. I mentioned my other job in Germany. She asked when I usually went there. Conversation waned and we sat glad the initial opening hurdle was behind.

Among the staff, and even with groups on site, we chose one night per tour to "dress for dinner". That had been mentioned in the brochure. Groups packed appropriately. I reminded her it would be tonight. Since she was the only guest, we wouldn't insist.

"Lance, I would like to. Give me a chance to present myself as more than a ragged beach comber. Delay dinner a half hour for me to assemble my armor."

"That's fine, I doubt there will be much jousting tonight."

Two hours later I was nursing a lemon soda and looking for the moon from a bar seat. A rustle of the hedge presented a vision with a very sexy smile. She had every reason. Low cut, open shoulders and short-skirt would get no sand in it. I compared it in my mind to her first-used thong. A mistake, I had to revise my location on the stool. My immediate thought was how 'no-bra' improved a swim suit. She had worked wonders on her hair considering the humidity. I hurried over to her with the mosquito repellant. I wanted nothing to interfere with her joy in being dressed that way.

We sat at a table and the staff sat wherever they wanted. Several sat themselves with her in the corner of their eyes. This dive-limiting drinking could be a drag. She was an enigma, much to be unearthed.

We took our soft drink up to the balcony and the staff disappeared to their cabanas. She sat close to me and we searched the skies for a while. She gently took my hand.

"Lance, will you still be able to dive with me tomorrow?"

"Of course! I've been behaving my drinking all day to be prepared. Do you have some area you would like to explore"?

Her smile suddenly reset to devilish as she replied. "Lance that could be a loaded question. I'll let you off the hook only this time. Explore the East reef!

A pause! I did not need any pause.

She quickly followed up, too late, the flirt was set. She would like to go to the East of the island where the licensed divers went the other day. And Lance, if it's necessary, here is my dive instructor's license.

After all I had seen her do, I had not noted that. I should have guessed she was beyond a novice diver. She had saved her partner innumerable times, right in front of my eyes. Then, the foray to 100 feet. Actually, that was probably more of a disqualification. All her help with re-setting equipment on the boats would pay her penance. At long last after searching in Spain, Germany and the Mid-West, I had found my partner. Ironically, after all the effort, she just appeared. If she was interested?

The next evening, I put my arm around her. There was no stopping a kiss. She moved in closely molding her mostly naked body to me. We were not exploring now. There was no holding back. The kiss continued with whispers and finally the French. We went from a brush to a passion to an attack. Down at the bar

Alexa played the "Unchained Melody". There is an emotional body-clock that chimes when you know you must stop. At least the first night. Our clocks were close to exact. I moved my lips reluctantly away. She put a big wet one on me and feathered over my cheeks and face.

"Lance, don't wear your wet-suit tomorrow. We won't be playing below the thermal clime. Speedos should be enough. I'll want to see your license."

She quickly rose disappearing into the dark.

I sat for a while, wondering if this had really happened or if it had been a dream. My German Cassandra crossed my mind. I knew there was nothing better nor poorer. It was style. I could never force an end to Denya's family and career. The third-grade teacher would collapse. Melissa was living another financial world.

CHAPTER SIXTEEN

Vanna and Lance Submurged Intent

>There are many ways besides a signature to signify continuing intent<.

We didn't hurry to get started. We needed no boat or staff help. We had a tank caddy and put our equipment on it making it easier to jockey it to the point we would gear up and submerge. I was wearing my speedos as commanded. I also wore a t-shirt to reduce the pressure of the tank against my back. She had the t-shirt as well; the thong was the one described on her first boat dive. For a while I avoided thinking about that. I mean I had high hopes, but for a while her licensed Captainship was calling the shots. I had my license laminated in plastic. Whatever might happen, I was heartened by the fact that she was a "kick-ass" professional diver. The job was advertised on the back of the bar.

She floated over to me, regulator suspended; snorkel affixed. She took my hand, pulled me off my feet and hand-in-hand we sculled out to the deeper part of the reef. We arrived at the hill of reef that boded the coming of the valley on the other side. I watched her skill in maneuvering in the small current that washed us. Her judgement was flawless and I am a professional judge of that. Her license was not a photo-copy of some nefarious dangerous diver. I had seen those, too. Sent home on the next plane.

As further proof, she basked in the sand waved up as a ray made its escape, inspired, no fear. She avoided putting her hand in any cave that could have an eel that wouldn't enjoy being wakened. There was a depth of experience here. A half hour on the tank of this and we floated to the third valley. We dropped to 20 feet of the 30 there and she stopped our progress. She floated up until we were mask to mask. She made the contact and we pantomimed a wet kiss. She turned me upside down so I could pantomime fun for her sliding the thong away. While I was so involved, the speedo fled. I could hold my breath for a long time. It turned out she could, too. Yup, licensed. She was no longer exploring when she turned us around, still limber and she slipped herself onto the unavoidable projectile. I knew the time-limit of this for a woman, in short order, much of my tank was empty. That is, both my tanks. I guided her to the surface where I promised I would return the favor.

"We'll see if you are as good as your word."

I took her hand, this time, firmly, and we skittered on the quick side up to my cabana with A/C. Seldom did you have a day with her that you didn't need it. Out of the water, anyway.

"I promised you something in the water after you drove me to salty ecstasy. Equality is the driver, it's your turn first."

She responded, "lover, you have a license for this?"

I ignored her and turned her upside down. More comfortable and sensitive out of the water. We spun through wind-mill turns before we fell into the post loving moments of vulnerability. A/C helped but no need to dress. Women may get tired of men adoring so earnestly. But, I'm sorry. No, I am not sorry.

Resting my gaze on Vanna, my mind was running pictures of different futures before my eyes. As most women could, she knew there was something behind that gaze. Eventually, she knew she could and would find out the source.

CHAPTER SEVENTEEN

Contract For Vanna

"Vanna, the desire you are unearthing at the moment is challenging my concentration. I could lay it out and disastrously offend you. There is no doubt about how we feel about each other?"

"Lance, Mr. Dork, have you not witnessed my response to you. I knew how I felt about you since the first day you helped me adjust my tank. I am much attuned to the value of a touch. I am not an unexperienced 18-year-old girl with stars in my eyes and no maturity in my soul. I can see your arousal endlessly. I am never impatient at the time you spend watching me. Nor will I ever if it comes to that. I have no doubt. I knew what I desired when I decided to extend my stay. You're such a gentleman, you probably didn't catch on until I pecked you on the cheek and asked you to dive with me. The nature of the dive was in my mind before I slipped my thong on that morning. Get the long-belabored point?"

"Vanna, I will surge ahead trusting in your response. I will go to the bottom line of what I desire. When I get there, please give me a chance to re-phrase anything that offends. I will try to be clear."

"Vanna, I would like you to stay here indefinitely as my partner and my lover. We would live in the little air-conditioned bungalow when we are here. Together. Any package deals or resort policies that affect you are burned. Any household things you want to bring down, I will negotiate shipping on a banana boat. What may be the most difficult is to decide how we will get a salary. There is no question in my mind that your skills are well above those of the present water staff. I would be surprised if there weren't many other experiences you have to bring to bear on our operations. I would need to get your thoughts before we, you and I, get something fair."

"I mentioned my job in Germany. I limit my time there as much as possible. It often goes two to three months. I cannot imagine being there without you that amount of time. I have an apartment there where we would live most of the time. Any other living would be in a hotel or perhaps a night or two with my dear friends, Greg and Cheryl, in Munich. Can we live with these parameters keeping our options open about marriage?"

"Lance, you must have been staying up late at night thinking about all this. My response is "yes". My passport is good for four more years. Since I am not a citizen here, I should not be on the payroll. We can explore options. The previous time I had in Germany was in closed, restricted places. To see more of it would be wonderful. I also can read your mind about what you worry might offend me. We know each other and neither will be trafficking the other."

Vanna continues, "I feel silly in even mentioning that. In fact, I'm looking forward to honing some of my skills in that area. Oh, we can make that one of my contractual demands if you feel you have too many of your own. Are we done yet with the contract? We are long beyond the end of our post-love non-lucid bubble time. Let's make a new one."

CHAPTER EIGHTEEN

Supply Trip and Rueger

We made supply runs to the mainland every two weeks. It was a two-hour ride if waves permitted and wind was not against us. Vanna went with me this time and weather was perfect. The bottom of the boat was not comfortable enough for loving. She dressed the island-girl outfit with short skirt, white lace along the bottom seam, white socks and tennis shoes. It had to be an industrial strength bra and the pinks appeared no matter what the blouse or top.

Vanna was an immediate favorite of everyone we saw. The owner of the supply store provided a money exchange service which gave a generous exchange rate and you could cash personal checks. I am a major customer and with Vanna on my arm, we had many invitations to tea or beer, sometimes Southern Comfort.

Life in the country had taken on a somber atmosphere due to the drug traffic and the deaths directly involved. It was on the mainland, but had migrated to the main island. My island was an hour and a half by boat on a good day from that island. Tourism there had taken a hit. I had never before considered safety other than air embolisms or nitrogen narcosis as issues in the diving world. News and friend's anecdotes made me reconsider. I went to a mainland sports store and found I could buy a pistol if I had the cash. I had one and when Vanna became dear to me, I got one for her. While the supply people were loading the boat, I showed Vanna what I had purchased. I asked if she had experience. She, too quickly in my mind, said yes! I was doubtful but knew there was a gun club a few hundred yards into the mountains. We could walk and did.

The target area had a sandstone cliff that would absorb any stray bullets. We were alone. I could comfortably; not hurriedly, set her up with the luger. I took a few shots with my Colt as she watched. I asked if she would like to try and she agreed. The targets were bulls-eyes thirty yards away. I had hit the target at some place each time. Vanna set her stance, raised both arms and fired. The bullet hit the outer rim on the right side of the target.

"Lance", she said, "I think this one is pulling to the right. Let me adjust the site."

Her next shot went into the left outer circle. She said, "Ok, I've got the angle for this gun at this distance."

She fired five more rapidly and hit the center every time.

I made a mental note: This woman manhandles heavy tanks and diving equipment, dives as an instructor, captains a huge dive boat, dives each time, and is the unseen 'diving buddy' for groups of six or more. She is a strong swimmer with live saving training. I had witnessed that as a twelve-year old boy panicked when his old model B.C. disconnected in open water. Now, to my mental checklist I had to add "crack shot".

The day had started sunny and our ride over was relatively quick. Walking back from the quarry, we were drenched in a summer squall. The wind came up. I had been here before. I hurried over to the supplier who was already unloading the boat. I quickly borrowed his pick-up and drove to the edge of town to reserve a room in the only decent hotel in the area. After a drenching, Vanna, in her sailor girl outfit, looked a succulent course. She was waiting in the lobby-bar of the hotel on the square which would not be one I would book. A few men were sitting around, playing cards and back-gammon. They weren't watching their cards much at all. I paid and immediately hurried her out. A quiet sigh of disappointment.

The boat would be secured to the dock. There would be no hard bottom to interfere with passion tonight. I had often recommended the hotel to divers missing the morning plane due to wind or storm. A bottle of imported champagne arrived as our night-cap.

59

CHAPTER NINETEEN

Shrimp Defense

We were going to leave for Germany in two more days. We invited Roberto for dinner. He was a trusted friend with power of attorney if needed while we were gone. Over the years he had been much more than that.

He was looking downtrodden when he arrived. We noticed immediately and pursued whatever problem before serving. I quickly offered a glass of his favorite scotch. "What is it, my friend?"

"You know, Lance, that I have a shrimp farm and a dolphin riding business."

"Been there."

You know my island base is infested with drug dealers, big money narcotics peddlers. Not peddlers, major shippers. Recently there has been a larger than normal influx of shady businessmen and their radicalized thugs. Since they bribe all the police and government employees, there is no law nor enforcement. They have three power boats. Big motors. Two go out and rip the shrimp out of the beds. This happens at least once per week. They load it into an even bigger motor yacht and take it to the mainland and sell it to the people who have been my customers for years.

I ask why they have changed suppliers. Some don't even speak.

Finally, a long-time friend explained that they have families. If they don't buy from Don J. Mondo Do, they may' lose track of their children'. There is no police nor DEA nor government protection. They are forced to buy or something terrible may happen to their family.

I have gone and talked to the police chief who 'guffawed' me out of his office with arrogance and smirks. "We'll look into it", is the answer.

Absolutely nothing happens. I have gone to mainland authorities for the same smirk. And the same nothing happens. I keep going higher and they are all in Don J. Mondo's pocket. I don't have proof, but I am certain even the president is corrupt.

"I have no other place to go. I am going to lose my shrimp business. The dolphins don't make enough to pay the bills. The utilities bills to me have been tripled. Do you have any ideas? I'm dying!"

"Roberto, I do have a couple of ideas. I'm leaving to Germany in two days, but can do some research before I go. Any action I can take will have to wait until I return. I will try to limit the time in Germany as best I can."

Lance: "We can't solve it tonight. Meet Vanna and let's eat and maybe drink more than usual. I'm not diving tomorrow, tank anyway."

"Roberto, because I am gone to Germany, doesn't mean nothing is happening. From here on in, don't ask me what I am doing or not doing. Its better you don't know. Trust in our friendship and that I care and to my limit of power, I will help. Now via con Dios."

CHAPTER TWENTY

Vengeance by Night/Shrimp Fields

Later that night I spoke to Vanna.

"Sweetheart, if I am going to help Roberto, I could use your help. There is some danger involved. I will try to limit it, but I will love you the same either way, whatever you decide. I wasn't aware of the seriousness of this when I made your contract. I had only heard a couple snippets from Zulinda, who evidently was underplaying it."

"Lance, tell me the plan?"

"I don't have it completely figured out, but I don't think we can take Don J. Mondo Do openly. Whatever we do, we must avoid it being traced back to us. It could lead to losing my resort to fire or whatever he might plot."

"I think the weakness in Do's operation, or his crony's, is with the smaller boats doing the night raids. The larger boat that extorts the restaurants may also be a doable target."

"There are two things we could do to start to sting him tomorrow night. We will need the cordless re-breather systems and the two small one-person under water diver transports. I have the transporters docked under water on the west side of the island near the gravel airport. No one should know I have one nor were. The re-breathers are on the top shelf in the tank room. Have you used these?"

"I have used the re-breathers extensively. I have played

around with the transport but not seriously."

"Every-day I'm finding out more of what you can do. We need to have a big talk one of these days…. maybe in Germany."

"Tomorrow night, after dark, we attach the diver transports to the smaller rescue boat. We attach the small, quite electric outboard to the transom. Full black dive suit, two underwater lights and two variable crescent wrenches. Two pairs of pliers; a dive knife. Black plastic camouflage to cover the safety boat. Only for major emergency, put your Luger, loaded, in a plastic sack."

"Here is what we do. The boats have 100 horse motors. They will be outboards. Two, one for you and one for me. We must do this as quickly as possible."

"I'm going to guess you know what a pliers, a crescent wrench, a drive shaft, a cotter key, and a shear pin are?"

"You're right. I have no experience, however, of firing a pistol from underwater to a land-based target. I could throw a knife."

Muted shock in my eyes, I responded, "If we should have to fire a pistol, we will be out of the water and probably diving behind trees to save our skin."

"Let's go inside with the A/C, less apt to be heard. One other thing we will need is a small part of a centimeter measure. Are you still sure you want to risk this?"

"I am not prone to changing my mind after I commit, but continue with the plan."

"We drag the transports behind the security boat, boat covered in black, we in black full wet suit and black charred cork on our faces. Using the electric motor, we go to about one-quarter mile from the bay where the boats are moored. There we moor dropping anchor.

There is one support you are unaware of. A mutual friend of Roberto and I is an adjunct officer with the U.S. military stationed near the extra-long Cuenca airport. His field is drone management. We had a dinner with him and he showed us some things he probably shouldn't have. At the time I never dreamed that I would need him for protection. I called him after Roberto explained his worries. He will be a major protection for us. Except for a serious life and death situation, he will only provide intel. Roberto is ready to trust him with his life. In an emergency he might help. His call sign on this military radio here is "Songbird". Ours is "Birdcage." I'll alert him at the half-mile point."

"At the quarter mile point, we anchor the boat, discharge the transports, and ride in underwater. It should take ten minutes one way. We'll have another ten minutes to remove the shear pins and measure them, down to the smallest millimeter length you can read. Measure especially length and diameter. Make note of any anomalies. I'll measure and wrap the ropes mooring the boat around the propellers, just on my boat. I'll come back in my transporter to get you and we'll leave as we came. That is the basic plan. I'll check with Songbird at noted points to see if there's any reason to abort."

"If you need any directions on how to remove and replace the shear pin ask me now."

"I'm fine on the shear pin. I'll keep my hair under the suit hoody."

"I think that's all for tonight. If you are still ok on this, let's go to sleep. We'll have a 24-hour day tomorrow. Or, if you are feeling some stress, I could do something for you to get you to sleep easier."

She answered after dropping her hand, "I think I am ok, but you surely aren't."

"I'm always like that with you around."

"I deeply appreciate that. Come here now. An easy one, don't try to do a fifteen-minute marathon."

I stretched muscles and rose. Stretching Yoga has applications other than street fighting rapists. She pulled me down, midriff up, captured, and took me home, her eyes flashing. I ignored duration and flew free. It surely wasn't five minutes; no marathon. I caught my breath and laid down beside her.

"Lance, I changed my mind, short but complete."

I went quickly to her lips, bursting passion, dropped to her breasts. Lips on one and warm palm on the other, she held her breath. I skipped the midriff but thighs landing on swelling fire. Ragged breath, the A/C was on and she bested it with sweet vibrato middle C. A sweet success-announcing sound.

Lance breathes, "We'll be getting back to this tomorrow night."

"Lance, there will be a changing of mind. About the marathon, that is. Please be careful. We could be easily caught under surprise wilting fire tonight."

The wind had increased into the one-digits We arrived at the anchor spot in an hour. We had left at 1 a.m.

"Songbird, this is Bird-cage. Do you read?"

"Five by five, captain." He knew me well, but anonymity was the word of the night.

"Do you have infra-red up? Any warm spots? Over."

"Negative, I 've been monitoring the spot for two hours. I think they ran a robbing raid before midnight and are home drunk. I'm watching for thugs, though. Check back 10 minutes into the mission."

"Roger, over and out for about 15 minutes."

Vanna had her hair hidden and we made short work of disconnecting the transport. We had our tools and gun over our shoulders as the electric motor kicked in. Removal with measuring took five minutes, too long. Total thirty minutes.

Our B.C.'s was empty, we made no waves. No warning from Songbird. A bit of luck. Vanna's eyes were tense, business, combat wary in every direction. She well realized the delay and was prepared for a violent response. Dumb luck which couldn't happen again. We would be back here.

Our B.C.'s was empty, we made no waves. No warning from Songbird. A bit of luck. Vanna's eyes were tense, business, combat wary in every direction. She well realized the delay and was prepared for a violent response. Dumb luck which couldn't happen again. We would be back here.

CHAPTER TWENTY-ONE

Mondo Threat, Demise

In the middle of the second week after the swipe at Don J. Mondo's poaching boats, Songbird called.

"We have three intruders approaching your pier arriving in probably fifteen minutes. Three aluminum boats. Over."

"Roger that, we have two of them on surf reader."

Vanna went down the hill to my right, Weatherby hidden. I was at the bar with a pistol on a shelf, shotgun concealed under the fruit.

Don J. Mondo Do was maintaining a place between the intruders. Cowards foment insurrection, don't ever lead it. Here's a guy who knows he owns the police, gendarmes, lawyers, judges, the Senate, and other officials above and below. He can do and kill whoever he wants in Times Square and drink to it with champagne.

"Songbird, Mondo is coming toward me among the others. He has a shotgun. One henchman is in a clearing below where Vanna is standing. The other is 20 meters to the right of the first also in a clearing. They both have American assault rifles."

"Roberto, get over behind and below Vanna. Unless she misses, don't give away your position. If I get into trouble at the bar, you have to save me. Put a wall of lead in front of the bar. I'll be cowering low behind it, in the fruit cellar. There's a guy with an assault rifle up from you behind Vanna. She knows it."

"Vanna, Mondo's got a shotgun. If that comes up, it's my problem. You shoot the guy up the hill, duck and take the guy in front of Roberto. Roberto will cover if you have trouble, but I'd like to depend on your speed in the first volley.

"Birdcage, we have them on screen, guns also. If the least happens, they will go to jail for illegal weapons. But there is no sheriff nor judge. Protect yourselves. We have the green lens operating, say burst if you feel you are about to get shot."

'Songbird, if a shot is fired, Vanna will take the one out downhill from her. You MUST take the one nearer me in the clearing. If I say burst, it will be because Don J. Mondo has leveled an obvious threat at me, my business or my workers and families. I will surely say "burst" and dive below the bar. Be right on top with finger on your trigger. A second late and I'm dead. You can't mistake or think about the fading democracy. His shotgun will injure or kill me even behind this one plywood thickness of the bar. Please don't hesitate! Over"

"Roger, we know our business! Over."

The green lens was the killer option. Nobody but Vanna and I had any possibility of seeing it.

"So, Mr. Starr, maybe it's the former Dr. Starr! We meet at last."

I said nothing, meeting his glare.

"I've had a few accidents with my shrimping boats recently. You wouldn't know anything about that, would you?"

"Why would I know anything about that? As far as I know, you have no shrimp farms."

"Ah, Mr. Starr. That is where you are wrong. On my island, if I want a shrimp farm, I take a shrimp farm. The easy or the hard way. I will take the dolphin business if I want it, too."

Again, I said nothing hoping Songbird was recording.

"You don't leave clear tracks, but I know you are causing these delays. Late delivery of shrimp can cause spoilage. I don't tolerate losses."

"There are courts who indicate ownership in a civil matter. Take it to them."

"No, Mr. Starr, on this island I am the authority. The police and courts are manned by people who agree with my claim. I am also the judge and jury on what is now your late island, here. You are guilty of damaging my shrimp farm equipment and will not have a chance to do it again."

The shotgun came up, I yelled "Burst' and dived behind the bar, head into the fruit cellar. The BOOM, and I grabbed my shotgun and rose to whatever might be developing. The remains of the top left of the bar were tatters. The only shots I heard were from Vanna's Rifle.

Songbird beat Roberto to the draw. No, it was Vanna. Songbird's burn had come in seconds too late. I was alive because of Vanna. She had taken three out in a matter of three seconds at 180 degrees apart.

Peeking over the bar, I saw Mondo on the ground, a small plume of smoke under his chin. One rifle, one drone. There was no trace of blood. His gun had flown over his head. His face was set in surprised rictus.

I hurried to hug Vanna and thank her for saving my life. Her shots had been perfect. I also checked to secure the passing of the victim of the green flash.

"Roberto, I need you over here ASAP, for sure now. I need help."

"Lance, I'm back in the channel, didn't even get a shot off. Will be there in ten."

Roberto was in shock seeing Mondo deceased.

"Roberto, he and his henchmen tried to kill us. Between us,

we managed to survive. The fact that you didn't get a shot off doesn't mean you weren't a critical life saver, particularly for me. I need your help to dump their three aluminum boats, and their bodies."

"I need you to devise something that will sink those bodies and keep them down for several years. We'll see if Songbird can help with the boats."

Roberto responds, "We'll attach the U.S. armaments, guns and ammo to Mondo, et al. The water out north east of the island is over 400 feet deep."

"Songbird, this is Birdcage, over. We have three aluminum boats to move north-east out of sight and circulation. They are empty of any cargo. If we pull them over to the east of the island, can you drill some holes and light the gas tanks?" Over!

"Birdcage, there are no bodies in them?"

"Songbird. I am unaware of any bodies. For sure not in them."

"Ah, very interesting, your short memory. Maybe it's shock. We'll deep six the boats. Bring them right now. I don't want to face being late for dinner. Out!"

"Vanna: "Can you go over to those ruined engines right away? Take any Styrofoam out so they sink fast, and stay sunk. I want what scum remains on the mainland or Roaban to know any threats or actions they make to hurt will be met by huge repercussions. I want to do it immediately on the day they sent their "Mondo". I want him to disappear on the same day that their damaged engines disappear. I don't want them to use them again to destroy us. Tow them over outside the north wall beyond what the tourists can see or hear and Songbird will make them vanish."

"If any of you folks think I'm a little unhinged here, remember I came within 3 seconds of being killed 20 minutes ago."

"It continues to be urgent that we leave no evidence, and

move fast. Vanna, maybe it would be better if I come and we do it together, or if you are concerned, I can do it alone. I will check with Songbird, but don't expect much extra security from them."

"Lance, what part of 'I'm not going anywhere without you and you ain't going anywhere without me.' Do you not understand? Given a half hour, I can destroy those bodies and boats beyond any recognition."

"Thank you. My lifesaver of tonight. We need to complete this because tomorrow we need to meet with Zulinda from the other resort. I think we'll need her help because that larger boat continues to poach shrimp two or three days a week."

After dispatching Don J. Mondo and his cruel crew, Vanna and I briefed Roberto and Songbird about our now delayed, but pending return to Frankfurt. With the need now for a new Don J., we should be able to do what we needed to and get back before they were re-organized.

CHAPTER TWENTY-TWO

Enter Rayban Hernandez

Rayban Hernandez was by far the richest young man in Sambo Creek on the Northwest coast of Central America. It was a bitter-sweet reality. His dad, Octavio was an icon to him as he was growing. He was the man who taught Rayban to fish. He taught many other things that had to be shared to feed the family. Rayban had a younger brother, Octavio Jr. and his mother worked as housekeeper and cook for one of the banana management families. Rayban was too young to realize the survival struggle of the family, a time when Dad had to catch fish every day to put food on the table. When Ray reached age 13, mom got the housekeeping job and together they bought a moderate fishing boat. No longer forced to fish with plastic-line from shore, there was time to offer guided tours to men who came from the U.S. with big money. Dad knew the waters of the Caribbean after forty years. Boat tours were offered as well. There was no option; Rayban had to work on the boat. And that's where he got his name. His name was really Francisco. Initially people called him Paco. One of the tourists forgot his sun glasses on the boat. They were wrap-around and Paco never went out without them. The RayBan sun glasses became his name, Rayban.

Occasionally, Rayban's father had to travel to the capital to fight the drug lords of the Bay Islands and northern coast. This fight wasn't yet of the bloody type, but the lords through bribed lawyers and judges persisted in raising taxes and increasing commercial fishing license costs on all but the drug lord's lackeys.

Not paying a bribe to the lords, small businesses fought a losing battle at least in the short run. Octavio hated the trip for this but it was the only thing to keep his family functioning. He also distrusted flights being flown into the country's Capital. The runway was perfectly acceptable for a DC-7. To accommodate the larger 727's and 737's, a runway bridge had to be built over an existing highway. Years of graft had siphoned huge sums out of the government by the drug cartels. Needed renovation lagged and many other places were becoming dangerous, as well. Even with that, pilots had to approach at minimum speed and flare out to get down in available time. Fog often exacerbated the difficulty. The dependable DC-3's and 5's only flew the north coast routes. Buses were often more dangerous. They were seriously overcrowded, sometimes fell off narrow mountain roads, and frequently were forced to stop by lord thugs and the people robbed of all possessions.

This day Octavio flew. He always bought flight insurance. If the worst happened, at least his family would be taken care of. The combination of worst-case conditions, high level wind, ground fog and wet runways developed causing the worst catastrophe. Getting low enough lost the minimum seconds needed to get to flare. Octavio's plane crashed onto the road bridge below and he was in front of the wing. Below the front of the wing, there were no survivors; neither the pilots.

Rayban returned at sundown with a full locker of fish and two well-heeled sport fishermen. Unusual, there were scores of people on the city dock. Rayban jumped to the pier, secured the boat and turned into his mother's sobbing arms. His brother was standing there in shock, tears streaming.

"What?"

"Francisco, your father was on a 727 airplane that crashed at the capitol airport at noon today. There were some survivors at the back of the plane, but Dad was in the front. Rescue workers found some of his belongings, but he had passed." Rayban gathered his remaining family in his arms and his mind relived Dad helping him learn to ride a bike, play a large fish, prepare fish, handle a boat and on and on, a lifetime.

Survival left little time for grieving. Legally, there was only twenty-four hours to perform the funeral ceremony. Rayban went fishing or touring only half days for a week. He stood near his mother as friends came from all over to "give you my sincere condolences". He was sick of hearing that over and over. The numbers waned and his mother could suffer her grief alone and with the two boys. Sores would begin to heal as much as they could and there would be some other old woman or man appear with "condolences", reopening the wound in my mother's soul. He could see the shivers moving through her face and the drooping of her shoulders. When you learn of a death, if you can't avoid going to it, get it over with, and discard those meaningless words. Use other words. Ask about the future, plans, changes, things that should now be considered. Help with the future is the only you can give.

Two weeks after the death, a cartel crafted silk suit appeared at Rayban's door, pure imbecilic lieutenant. From torture to bittersweet moments, he informed us of the one-million-dollar flight insurance my dad had purchased.

"Sign this form and we will calculate the expenses and taxes and deposit the remaining proceeds in your bank account."

He might as well have said, "Bribes" as expenses.

I had observed my dad fighting these crooks. For years. The lords, early in their coup of the government had re-instated death tax. Of a million dollars, they would change the law again against my father's will.

"We will sign nothing today. Give me your card and I'll call for an appointment."

Friends and clients had often urged me to get a lawyer if anything of any value to the druggies should develop in my life. I knew my father's lawyer and family. They lived in the suburb of Pedro Sula. I called and heard a cry of grief. A more measured voice took the phone. It was Felipe, my dad's old friend's son. I told him who I was; he knew immediately. We had been classmates in high school. He also had read about the life insurance. He knew I had a large inheritance coming. I told him that I had called to retain his father's help with the will and particularly how to protect the large sum. I learned of the cry of grief. Felipe's father had been on the same plane. Our old friend and lawyer, gone.

"Rayban, you still have a lawyer if you would trust me. I graduated from LSU law school and passed the bar exam for the U.S. and here. After passing the bar, I worked in a law office in Atlanta, 'Jones, Crawford and Race' as an intern. Being black is still a problem there, as you have probably experienced here. I guess a conquistador got in the mix with some green-eyed beauty of a great-great grandmother. My DNA black is dark brown. As sick as that is, the green eyes and the good wardrobe my dad could supply disguised my Afro-American roots. I eventually worked my way up to a trusted level in the firm.

I was aghast at the corruption and dodges of law they practiced. Bribery was the name of the game. Corruption is rife in the U.S. system if you get into bigger money. They call it Lobbying. It is more expensive than it is here even with the drug lords attacking us.

A corrupt president pardoning his white-collar lackeys up north. We never learn the prices and favors that pass in the smoked filled back rooms. I came under scrutiny from my own firm because I avoided this. Using the excuse of my father's death, I am now back here. I am still on what's considered "good terms" with them, but I can't imagine what favor I would ever ask of such racist, evil people."

"Well, Rayban, a disturbing story for someone offering to be your lawyer, but that brings us up to date."

"Felipe, could you estimate the costs I would need to provide for you to do several things. One, to avoid as much as possible damage the cartel could try to level at me, secondly, avoid any frivolous costs they could use against my business. Finally, get my million-dollar inheritance out of this country so no other taxes can be manufactured against me. What would you need? A fair price. I don't want to take undue advantage of our friendship."

"Rayban that's a tall order. I can't give a definite cost until I study some options, many actually. Unfortunately, that includes the U.S. while this president is permitted by the Republican Senate to abuse the laws of the constitution and even decency. I'm not sure I could solve this before he gets voted out. My guesstimate would be a retainer of $10,000 plus in the range of an additional $50,000. I would include the retainer in the $50,000, but dealing with a million dollars could take it above that. I will provide an item by item description and if there are options, would not carry them out without your pre-approval.

"Felipe, I am a fisherman with no university degree, but much expertise in the Caribbean. Enough to provide for my mother and brother well; for a family of my own as soon as finances, and the right girl comes along. You were an excellent student for the years we were together. I trust in the fairness that lives in our ethics between families.

I think, in the interest of avoiding taxes by showing investment and costs, I should find a much higher quality fishing and tour boat. Potential tax expense deductions. The boat my father fought and saved for a lifetime, was surely a big step forward for our family. I'm young enough to see the surging technologies and am capable of handling an excellent boat into that 21st Century world. If I should be cheated out of my money by U.S. bribery or local drug lord licenses, I would at least have that and the fine living it could provide."

"Felipe, I would like to move on that as soon as possible. Before any corrupt cartel or corrupt government can block me. However, I would like any financial guidance you might have considering all the other technicalities before I make the purchase."

Without putting any local collateral in jeopardy, Rayban visited north coast marinas and some on the Pan Handle of Florida seeking the right price but also the most advanced technology. On the internet, he found one in the Cayman Islands. Felipe knew the abnormal private account activities of this island. His Atlanta law firm had been frequent clients. He drew up detailed contracts and bill of lading to secure the purchase.

CHAPTER TWENTY-THREE

Starr Resort Communications Center Attack on Rayban, East of Guanaja

With monthly visits to Zulinda, our exotic resort neighbor, we operated business as usual. Three months went by with no harassment nor anything else.

We settled into an evening of "no-dive" planned for tomorrow. A couple extra drinks on the veranda. We were beginning to move off to our lover's bedrooms when the emergency radio channel blared. There was a cruiser to the east of Guanaja out of control.

We ran down to the bar to communicate by emergency radio. We called with no response. I went to the dive boat to use radar technology to locate the call. We continued calling and after 10 long minutes, we got a response. It was Rayban from Sambo Creek, who all but Vanna knew because of his beautiful new boat. He wasn't lucid.

He garbled, "Thief, attack," stopped.

His voice, "Concussion. I'm lost." Other wounded sounds with pain.

Vanna called, "Lance, you have him on radar? Is that the guy from Sambo Creek?"

"Yes, his name is Rayban and his cruiser is the "Octavio.""

"The radar is on the dive boat. Let me get the radar up on

the rescue boat. Get three more people down here, and Vanna, get the pistols and ammunition."

We loaded up with emergency items. Vanna drove the boat and I followed the radar. A boat captain repeated calls time after time. Garbled messages flew through. He tried to give us his location.

I said, "I know exactly where he is." I handed the luger to Vanna and pushed the Colt into my waistline.

"Rayban, are you alone?"

"Alone, please help, I'm dizzy!"

"Rayban, are your lights on?"

"Red top, red pot, red...."

"Say again Rayban?"

"Vanna: Call Songbird and see what they have."

Lost in the ether, "Starr, I think I see you on my radar."

"Songbird, this is Birdcage. Call sign "Birdcage please. We have an emergency call from a boat registered to a Rayban. It's the Octavio. Can you locate?"

"Birdcage, this is Songbird. We have the Octavio. We have you, also. Unable to see what emergency is from here. You are less than 30 minutes out. Over."

I grab the rail for balance. Lance throttles down and I drop buoys and secure the two boats together. I start on board the boat and Lance warns me to let him go first. That's a non-starter and I leap aboard with my hand on my Luger. The only thing I see is Rayban, on his knees, head between them. Lance joins me with a concerned chauvinistic smirk, but quickly scans the rest of the boat. I focus on Rayban.

"Songbird, this is Birdcage. We are aboard Rayban's boat. It's very new. Ray has a concussion, but there is no sign of loss of blood. Unless he has something internally. He's dizzied, but improving.

"Vanna, I shudder to ask, but did you also have nursing along the way?"

"I worked as nurse on a battleship for six months."

"Now don't tell me you are a doctor, too?"

"I took a lot of anatomy in undergrad, but didn't go to medical school. Parents couldn't afford it and I couldn't stand five more years in school."

"Can you see if Rayban has a concussion, or something else?"

"I know that. Sailors get them frequently on low gangway ships."

She raises his body to see into his eyes, which are closed. She takes my light and opens one eye, shines light, watches, and opens the other similarly. She runs her hand over his arms and legs and feels on the stomach. She double checks the neck and upper leg.

"His eyes are dilated, but mildly responsive. He has a brutal concussion, but he is fighting back. There is no noticeable internal bleeding. We can move him onto his back, but no more movement. He needs quiet rest, so don't try to ask him a lot until I see more activity. It will take at least a half hour, but we should have one of the captains keep a constant watch."

We wait. I go through the boat from engines to stern seeing only some scratching from force on the fish off-loader. No, it is forced and is still open.

"Songbird, this is Birdcage, over."

"Standing by, Birdcage?"

"Songbird, the captain is here and presently alive. Vanna notes a brutal concussion but some mobility returning. His eyes are closed and show dilation anomalies. He tried to speak on-route but it was garbled. No bleeding other than a scratch on his head where somebody hit him with something. Vanna and I agree he needs to be treated by a doctor. The closest available is the company one in Cuenca. Vanna can take our security boat and I think I can manage his. It's new it may take itself. There is some damage indicating theft in the fish unloader, but that won't impede movement. I will run this full out if it doesn't irritate his body. You could try to get a doctor to meet us, but the only ones I know are in the drug lords stable and I doubt they will bother because Rayban is a capable competitor. Call the hospital directly to prepare them to meet us."

"Roger, Birdcage, out!"

"Vanna, let's get him on a cushion with his feet up. I want to run as fast as possible and there is a chop. We need the cushion to absorb the vibration."

"Roger, that. Do you want me in the other boat? The captain can continue to observe here."

We ran at 23 knots for forty minutes before he stirred. We were another hour out. The security boat was having trouble but followed our running lights. I slowed and got Vanna back on the cruiser with Ray. The captain ran the security craft.

Occasionally he tried to talk but lost his breath.

"We got, "attacked, dark, stole fish," and he faltered. Vanna caressed his forehead with cool water, but he was gone for another half hour.

"Songbird, this is Birdcage, over."

"Birdcage, we have both your boats on radar. You are one half hour out. Roberto is ashore and will meet you at the banana boat dock. It is empty. You see a large liner off the dock? We have talked to the captain and he can't land for six hours; reducing port fees."

"Thanks, out."

Ten minutes later Vanna said, "His eyes are flickering, having trouble maintaining focus. Rayban, can you hear me? Lance, you should come here. He doesn't know me. I can handle the boat."

"Rayban buddy, can you hear me? It's Lance from Guanaja. He turned his head toward me and squinted finally getting focus. Rayban, this is Lance, can you hear me?"

"Yah, better than I can see ya."

"That's ok. You have a concussion. Vanna, my partner is a nurse. You'll be ok, but we are taking you to a doctor to double check. Rest now."

Rayban, anger, adrenaline driving him, "Lance, I can't rest. My boat was bordered by those drug thugs. They dumped my flounder into a net next to their boat. Somebody hammered my head and I went out. Their boat had no name as I could see. I tried to call Songbird, but collapsed. As I went out, the only thing I saw was a red can or coffee pot hanging on the diesel exhaust."

He didn't talk again as Roberto loaded him into his jeep. Vanna moored the boats away from where the banana boat would dock and I got a taxi to Sambo Creek to advise his family. They came right back with me. I dropped them off at the hospital and headed back to join Vanna. The younger brother, now a teenager went to the mooring with me and took the Octavio back to the pier in Sambo Creek.

Roberto called and said he would stay with Rayban until the next day, or whatever was needed.

"Songbird, this is Birdcage. The Octavio was boarded by drug thugs. The hold was off-loaded; stolen. He had flounder so I guess they took the catch up to Gulfport to sell at the wholesale market. They shouldn't have arrived there yet. Can you see them to confirm that? The only description we have is a red can or teapot hanging on the exhaust. Can you get in close enough to identify something like that?"

"Stand bye, Birdcage. We can identify the make and color of your girl's shoes. That's classified. No trouble with a teapot."

I was red-faced looking back at Vanna. "They'll pay with bruises at our next dinner."

"Birdcage, this is Songbird. You were correct on the heading of the pirates. We got the teapot and they are heading back to their liar on the big island. We have several identification marks on the boat. We may have to discuss any response. Things had been going well for quite a while. Maybe they got a new Don J. Do. Do you have any word on Octavio? Over."

Vanna answered, with anger in her voice, "Songbird, they hit Octavio very hard with an oar or something. His concussion is not minor. If he had fallen overboard, they would have smiled and let him drown. Did you tape your contact with the crook's boat? Oh, and keep your invasive little camera above my neck. Over."

CHAPTER TWENTY-FOUR

Repeat of Loyalty

The sun was up by the time we returned to the resort. The boat captain went to his bungalow. Vanna and I had a 'Bailey's and wrapped each other up, until 3:30 p.m. the next afternoon. Then we were quiet, wrapped and re-wrapped in several layers. She not so quiet.

A stunning wake-up call but even after, I could sense anger in Vanna. I rolled next to her in our usual emotional bubble.

"Vanna, tell me what is stressing you?"

She grits her teeth as she said, "Those bastards would have left him to drown. They left his engines engaged. Evidently this new design slips the boat into a circular trajectory when there is no sense of push or pull in some pre-programmed circuit. Barring that, it could have crashed on a reef or rocky shore and exploded and burned."

"Lance, I was internally hesitant when we first fought back at the druggers, sinking their boats and killing them. I participated but felt some guilt. I had left jobs of similar violence, perhaps because I hadn't been personally convinced of the worth."

"The personal value became abundantly clear as Don J. went after you with his shotgun. I was watching; everything changed. At that second, I had no doubts. My response was drilled in, habit, not thought. After his atrocity to Rayban, I held him in my arms, my personal arms. He was in serious shape. I didn't indicate any of the things I was doing to treat him. We could have lost him. It was touch and go all the way to shore. Lance, if you have any doubts, I personally will lead a revenge strike. I now understand how vulnerable we could be if the lords get definite information about us. We have no choice but to leave no survivors nor evidence."

"Vanna, you saved my life tonight, come into my arms. There never was nor ever will be a doubt about you."

"I have been scheming and planning all night about what we can do. Let's wait until Songbird can send us the video. I think I have a plan we can mount the next time Ray takes a load of flounder north."

CHAPTER TWENTY-FIVE

Dinner in Sambo Creek,
Vanna Meets Rayban, Lucid

Two weeks after the rescue, Rayban had gotten through his dizziness and invited all of us including Songbird to a Sunday Dinner. Vanna and I came together leaving the two boat captains to cater to the 20 divers there for the week. Rayban's mother was busily scurrying around making hors d'oeuvres as starters while Rayban grilled large fish, some Sea Bass and some Sea Bream. He offered a fish-shish, which was a filet flounder deboned and twisted onto a skewer like a shish-kabab, onions and tomatoes impaled, as well. Fish-Kabob!

Roberto was there. I was reluctant to involve him in this revenge response, but with at least three bully pirates who would likely try a heist again, I needed the manpower. Vanna met Rayban for the first time out of concussion. We had an enjoyable dinner with Songbird being gentlemen and super accommodating with Vanna. Lots of fun, but she consistently dresses giving no escape for a male eye. Not Zulinda, but not an iota less dangerous. I could remember when I first met her trying to keep my eyes up. Songbird was struggling while I no longer had to get permission to ogle. She gave it back looking down, not up, at me.

After digestives, I politely wished Songbird good night and said we had some other things to discuss that perhaps they would be better not to hear. Kisses on both cheeks all around and Vanna, Rayban, Roberto, and I huddled away from mother and little brother.

I reviewed the information Rayban had remembered and that Songbird sent in the video. There was no doubt we would recognize this motley crew if we saw them, even in fog again. I laid out the plan for the next night that Rayban would be heading north. We couldn't necessarily wait for fog because these guys were on an evil run and flounder was big money. Rayban would advise us the day he would leave.

CHAPTER TWENTY-SIX

Vanna and Zulinda Tangle, Zulinda Wins Verbal, Vanna Wins Form

Rayban had three sport fishermen to guide, big money, low overhead. It was a week later he contacted me. He said he had a full catch, but had to take it north at night or the hot Caribbean sun would spoil it. The wholesalers bought mostly in the mornings, anyway. Advantageous for the pirates, but we would be prepared this time.

I asked Roberto to come over on the afternoon of our response. I asked him to bring a gun if he had one. He had several. I advised Songbird of our night journey. We napped in the afternoon. Octavio informed us of his departure from Sambo. Our resort was two hours into his journey. We began to radar monitor passing ship traffic.

CHAPTER TWENTY-SEVEN

Face-off: Zulinda and Vanna

Aware from the resort radio of the coming action, Zulinda appeared at the top of the path from her resort. They both knew her very well, in a sense loved her very well. Roberto was still there with Rayban returning to what he expected would be additional planning with Zulinda. Vanna faced me across the table, eyes burning. She immediately left. Zulinda was, as always, naked. She insisted that her clients mirror that, or leave. She modeled her signature behavior.

There was a pregnant pause after which I reviewed what we were planning. Zulinda had been here three years before I even started constructing Starr Resort. I had known her most of the last two years. Striking she is, I couldn't keep my eyes down every minute. It never went beyond that. As distracting as it was, she could have information useful to what we were doing. After a few minutes into my review, Rayban surely needed to prepare his boat. Likewise, Roberto suddenly needed to load his armaments. They had both been close with Zulinda, but were not immune to her presence.

In a personable way, eyes up, I introduced Vanna to Zulinda. Vanna had short shorts and bra under her top. The air crackled between them. I jumped to clarify more. Vanna is my love, camp leader, and my dear partner. She has saved my life and soul several times. Vanna, Zulinda is owner and operator of the Nude.com resort down through the jungle. She had been running her camp for several years before I cleared the hill for ours.

Zulinda commented, "three years."

"We have used the joint Cuenca supplier to improve efficiency which has improved our profits, but largely our security. With Zulinda's cooperation, we were able to clandestinely install the trip wires for what has become a much-needed security device."

The atmosphere cleared a bit when I introduced Vanna as my love. Anytime I said anything complementary about Zulinda, tension increased.

Zulinda followed, "By the way, I had Sandy return the unneeded wire and here's the refund."

"Thinking, now they're warmly chatting about a guy I know nothing about," Vanna quickly rose and went to the back of the cabin.

Before I could begin to discuss the cooperation, I needed with taking out the remaining trawler, Vanna returned. Nude, not even shoes. If I should try to describe the look in her eyes, I would be in trouble forever.

My speech halted, Zulinda stood and said, "Vanna, you are gorgeous. I could never have held a candle to you."

My heart in my mouth, Vanna took a breath and quietly responded, "Thank you."

Zulinda answered, "Vanna, I feel some tension between us. In my lifestyle that has happened before. It is obviously because I prefer not to dress."

But let me say this again, "You are beautiful hot, molten heat. Since you now will be with Lance, I would like to be friends with you, too."

Vanna, "I appreciate that, and I know you knew each other long before I arrived. You, too are lovely. It's impossible that some relationship didn't blossom with you two during that time. Are you about done?"

This was a blatant attempt to mark her territory.

Zulinda is no dummy. She stood and said "Yes". She started down her path, thought, returned and sat.

I had nothing to say about this. I was worried. "Vanna was deadly."

Zulinda said," Lance, we need to clear the air here, and it would be best if I do it, or at least start it."

She turned to Vanna and took in the blazing anger.

"Vanna, for many dangerous reasons here, we need to be friends. I want to open that door. I am not competition nor is your resort competition to mine. It's obvious you have either imagined some erroneous ideas, or feel endangered. You need to know some facts."

Vanna snapped back, "You mean about the three years you were here while Lance was building the resort or other times after that. I don't have to imagine. If that's what you want to say, forget it!"

"Vanna, your reaction is understandable. This time, it is mistaken. I heard Lance tell me you are his love. I have never heard those words about any other girl from him. That is evidence enough to put these worries to rest. We have never had a relationship develop that would include that. Over the years I have had two strong ones with men that enjoy my life style. I trust I will be testing that again, soon, not with anyone you know."

This wasn't only about a verbal clash for Vanna, she had disrobed to 'out-sex' Zulinda. Obviously, I picked up on that, and obviously I kept my mouth shut.

Zulinda struck back again harder than I had ever seen her. "You need to settle down and listen to me. I'm not going to leave here until this is fully communicated and you can do what you want with it, or him."

Zulinda continued, "My resort was growing and busy. I wasn't worried about our resorts being in competition. The whole auras are different. For two years, he never even visited my resort, never came over the hill. During his third year, the Cartel waited in hiding and over two months stole all his incoming supplies and mine. At that point, he came to suggest some ideas. This was the first time I even met him. I don't take strangers to bed."

"We agreed to share boat captains to jointly make and defend, if necessary, the incoming supplies from Cuenca. It was working; neither of us had to be directly involved. I didn't see him for another year. Later, a short time before you came, he stopped to coordinate other shipping business. He told me about his trips to Germany. I enjoyed that because my grandparents still live there."

"We agreed to formalize that and he now comes once per month to share any info regarding what we're facing here. For your edification, in every inter-camp meeting, he has been fully dressed and I have been fully nude. Our friendship is platonic and what we know of each other is only what I see when he is wearing the thick corduroy to protect himself from the barbed hill. I have come over three or four times outside of the formal meetings. We don't even share a drink. I come because he is reluctant to come to the nudist operation.

If you hadn't in anger, repressed your feminine wiles, you would've intuited I came tonight because I am concerned that Rayban is involved in a dangerous operation. Rayban is a man I am learning much about, both with and without clothes.

I am not interested in an apology. I can understand the conclusions you could draw. As I said in the beginning, I am interested in your friendship. If you want to say something more, let's do it, otherwise, act supportive in our challenges."

Zulinda waited for a beat, and turned down her trail.

CHAPTER TWENTY-EIGHT

LANCE SOOTHS

The eyes were not great but I took Vanna by the hand into the bungalow.

"Lance, why didn't you tell me about this?"

"It never crossed my mind. There is nothing notable to tell."

"Lance, you are interested in sex, feeling what you do with me, I assume you would at least have a casual tryst with such a tall beauty."

"Vanna, you have heard her Force's holy truth. If I know the real you, you'll at least, over a day or two, accept it and we'll forget what wasn't even there to remember."

"I don't usually comment on this, but I did have lovers for various amounts of time while I knew Zulinda. Before you. I wasn't crazy horny. All ancient memories. You also might note that to avoid any wallops from you, I am sending you to do any and all inter-camp processes with Zulinda."

"Finally, and before we rest and go to dinner, for me there was, between the barbs, some pleasant truths. I doubt under the circumstances you considered these on a resigned, rational level. Through the steam on the sidelines, I could see viscerally the fierce love thoughts you have for me and I for you. We have talked about this and are grounded in our love. Selfishly, it is a security that is good for me to see occasionally. Now, let's wrap up for a while, quietly, because we have a risky mission in the offing."

I said no more, she relaxed and also said no more. Caressing her along her midriff, brushing her breasts, I woke, stilled and laid in question beside her.

"It's time to go if you still feel like it."

She turned and with every unclothed inch took me into a kiss on the pillow that could have seriously delayed the mission.

94

CHAPTER-NINE

Project Flounder: Avenge Attack on Rayban and Flounder Theft

"Songbird, this is Birdcage in the resort. Project "Flounder" is underway. Expect Octavio in our waters in two hours. Could you inform us if anything is launching toward us from the Drug Island to our West? Over?"

"Roger that, but their boat may not be as fast as Octavio; may match your security boats speed. We may have to inform Rayban to coordinate his speed accordingly. Birdcage, stay off your radio, we will contact the Octavio. Maintain radio silence. This is shaping up to be a night of patchy fog. Evidently the thugs have a mole in the Sambo creek area tipping them off. Too much chatter may tip them off, over"

"Song bird, appreciate advice, but my security boat is a ringer. I brought it on a Banana Boat. It has a Chevrolet engine capable of up to 22 knots. Pirates are at around seven."

"Birdcage, careful, their boat was running 18 knots when it was empty on its way home last time. Out."

"Roger, tell Rayban all this, out"

Vanna, Roberto, and I were pondering using the ramp boat for more inertia, but it's not that fast. We'll have to use the security boat. Vanna, please get the pistols and shotgun.

Sometimes before these dangerous activities, Vanna and I get heightened emotionally and meet in heat wondering if it could be our last time. In the end, the physical and emotional stresses were greater after the event than before. It was more stress-relieving to celebrate it then. Roberto was there anyway. I didn't want to influence him to take a run down to see Zulinda at Nude.com. I needed him and his cruiser.

Octavio was about 30 minutes east of us and heading north when Songbird alerted us of a pirate launch.

"That boat has three thugs; our facial-recognition confirms the same crew. But, Lance, they are heading at 18 knots and will meet Ray more north than west of you. You need to leave now. I'm informing Octavio. Maintain radio silence. He knows you're coming. Be aware, we predict a fog bank stretching from one mile south of the contact point to a half mile north. We are providing friendly situational information and know nothing of what you may or may not be doing. Songbird, out."

"Pedal to the metal, Vanna."

Eight cylinders took us to flank speed in 15 seconds. The boat was one of the long thin canoe style crafts that frequented the Bay Islands, usually fishing or hauling freight. A similar delivered my supplies. It could not plane off, but the power increased the speed to 23 knots depending on wind and wave action. The wind was against us, but mild.

"Vanna, the fish conveying machinery is on the starboard side. We need to go to the port."

Songbird, "Birdcage, we estimate crooks will arrive 1 to 2 minutes before you. Give it all the propulsion you can. Crooks are sporting pistols and battering rams; one American assault rifle. Songbird, out."

Rayban had the same information and was trying to stay ahead, yet let us catch up from the southwest. The thugs were on a north/north east trajectory. Ray may have to carry the initial blows, but he would not be caught unaware and would fight to the death to project his Octavio. He had a knife but no gun.

"Vanna, I see the pirate boat. It has only second's lead. Roberto, boat hook in right hand, pistol in left. Don't forget your tiller."

"Vanna, hang on to the tiller, but access the shotgun. Yeah, keep your pistol in your belt."

"Vanna, bring the boat right in on Rayban's wake. Pirates have moved to three feet. One jumped off on the bow. One on the transom, one still maneuvering their boat. The one on the bow is moving toward Rayban, probably the one who cold-cocked him the last time. Rayban is aware, but with the height advantage, the bald guy may get the club down too soon. Vanna thumbed off a double tap. He staggered and Rayban drove the knife into his throat. Pushed off the starboard machinery side of the boat, he was fish food in the propeller of the conveyor.

Vanna was exchanging fire with the bald-winged guy hiding behind the transom. Roberto swung our parasail seat over to hit the buoy Ray had dropped to between the boats. I jumped aboard and baldy was in a crossfire, body parts soaring in several directions.

I popped up to check Vanna. The marauders boat was 30 meters port and 20 meters aft of her driving our security boat. Roberto had fallen back 40 meters with his 100 MERC whining to catch up. The thug was trying to control his steering but firing off pistol shots at Vanna and me, some going right between us. I could hear the whiz. Rayban was cursing, "Not my boat!" He began swerving it to avoid rifle fire. My balance swerved the opposite way.

"Vanna, you have the angle, I don't."

I could see the venom in her eyes as she raised the shotgun. I gave her half-hearted cover fire. She put the first slug right into the tubing forcing water vapor into the engine and diesel fumes out, flames licking. She immediately realized the danger.

Vanna, "Lance, Rayban, get out of here, full speed north. NOW! Roberto head EAST, pronto. Hurry."

The bald, blond guy was ducking from my cover fire. Vanna, rose up again and put the remaining slug into the base of the boiler. A fire licked at the blond. It bloomed.

In the Octavio, I screamed, "Vanna, get down and go flank out of there. Get away, go west, upwind! All it's got, 23 knots."

As she turned and pulled quickly away, I fired another double tap into the alien boat but saw only the holes and damage I had done with my pistol. One of Vanna's slugs had pierced the boiler which erupted with a whom. No other movement. Engine pieces peppered her waters.

"Songbird reacted, "Oil and gas on the water. Withdraw if you are anywhere nearby. Out!"

"Camp radio now".

I had heard all I cared to from Songbird. Better for the Republican lackey of Don J. Mondo not to hear.

Vanna erupted, "Every-one, the boiler is sinking. Set your autopilot and get down."

Ten seconds after her last word, a red, rushing circumference of water and fire breached the surface.

"Sitrep, everybody, Rayban and I are fine."

"Roberto here, I'm clear."

Vanna: "Had to dodge part of the flying transom, but it missed."

From "Songbird, FYI: the crooks ran their engine too far, too fast and the boiler let go. Will check for survivors."

Lance, "Songbird, we would surely confirm your sighting and conclusions."

"Interesting, Birdcage, one of the crooks blew up onto the bow of the Octavio."

Lance, "Songbird, missed that. Maybe he was knocked out and fell off. We'll see if he drowned. If he was wearing an American Assault Rifle, it would have taken him right down. This is deep water. Out!"

We knew he was already being digested.

Smelling more diesel and some gas, I washed Rayban's sodium-light over the wake. It was blue, white and sometimes pink. Some of the petroleum had surfaced after the explosion.

"Octavio, do you have any emergency flares?"

"Of course,".

"Get up to flank speed before you throw one back. "

"This is Lance, on camp radio. Check the surface of the water near you. If you see bluish tinges, drive directly into the fog bank to the north. Go immediately, schnell!"

"Vanna, how far away are you from me?"

"I haven't been able to see you in the fog for over five minutes."

"Ok, change your heading to north-east".

"Roberto?"

"I saw your running lights about three minutes ago, lost them. Am proceeding North, I see the end of the fog bank, over."

"Rayban, quickly take us north until we get out of the blue surface diesel fuel."

"Vanna, veer north, top speed. Everybody, if you are not five hundred meters into the fog, inform immediately. Otherwise, there will be a fire bloom around you in two minutes."

Vanna," In position",

Roberto, "Out of danger."

"Rayban, fire that parallel to the surface over the stern toward the south."

Crackling, cooking, burning, no such explosion as before. It continued hot for five minutes then broke up into small area fires. Detached blond hair floated below the surface.

Lance on Camp Radio, "All craft, carefully return to initial point of enemy contact? Take your torches and search the area for any bodies or any evidence that could be a problem for us. If you find something, come and get me from the Octavio."

After ten minutes the area was scoured; Vanna approached.

Lance next to him at the wheel, "Rayban, I don't think we need you anymore. If we think it necessary, we'll debrief when you return. Be clear about what happened here: Three men with pistols and an American assault rifle waving, pushed their diesel engines too hot for too long. Their boiler exploded leaving no survivors. Song Bird will confirm that. But Rayban, we have a serious loose end here. Do not try to take another load north until we talk."

"Roger," a hug, and I jumped into our boat, Vanna driving.

Roberto followed, calling, "Lance, over where the boiler exploded, burned blond hair. Other body parts remaining."

"Roberto, take some wire and wall blocks. Check for any guns or knives. The hair sank, I'll weight the other pieces."

Roberto, "Area is clear, with one exception. The red teapot."

"Thank our lucky stars you noticed that. Songbird saw it. We know we got the right assassins. It's going to be connected to the brick and follow the crook to Davy Jones Locker."

We arrived at dawn. With more light we scoured the boat and found some minor pieces that may or may not have been of any evidentiary value. Knowing Roberto had been feeling guilty about the fight at the bar, Lance called him over and expressed his appreciation for backing Vanna, saving her at one point and with a hug showed how much his protection of Vanna meant to him. He also whispered thanks for catching the red water pot, saying "you may have saved our booty on that one." He re-filled the tanks, Roberto peeling off to nap with Zulinda.

Vanna and I hurried up to the cabin and once inside wrapped our arms, drew deep breaths and still dressed, went to our knees and fell to the bed. Asleep in minutes. Shower would wait till morning till we had more energy.

CHAPTER THIRTY

Vengeance for Roberto's Shrimp Theft Loss

We had taken a small chip out of Don J. Mondo's shrimp theft and extortion gang, but more had to be done, and sooner, not later. That was why I shortened our time in Germany, and why I hurried to see Cheryl. I explained keeping the details vague should any trails lead Don J. Mondo to Europe. I did show her the measurements of the shear pins and contents of their composition. She knew immediately the hardest metal that would do significant damage to the whole drive shaft and gearing of a 100 horse outboard Motor. Titanium. She offered to make the pins of that. I had the tools in Frankfurt to do this as well. After discussion, we decided to have her cut them and mail them to me in standard German mail. Building in a cut-out for her if Donny J. came sniffing my way. Machines even from the same manufacturer leave different scratches not unlike fingerprints. I didn't want to make it easy for a Mondo technician to unearth a comparison. Cheryl made them and instead of mailing them, dragged Greg out of his trance to come up to Frankfurt for delivery and dinner.

He managed to last one night. They hurried him back to his big 'thinking' chair. Vanna and I stayed a few days more for German folk dancing, and Sauer Braten. I showed up in the Mercedes office in person for a couple days and Vanna topped up her wardrobe with garments that would only make it through one night or less with me.

Roberto had for many years been integral in covering for

me, finding equipment for me, and even in a military fashion, defending the resort with me. I didn't want to make him wait three months for relief. I packed the small cylindrical destroyers in a hidden check-in bag. Vanna and I spent the 12-hour trip looking at options to insert the destruction pins, and also break the back of the trawler that had extorted shrimp sales on the coast. She said she'd deal with it. These asides of hers reminded me we hadn't had the big chat in Germany

On the flight from Munich to Miami, I contacted Roberto, gave our itinerary, but asked him not to see us nor call us after we arrived. No direct contact, nothing on sea coast radio. I didn't specify. He knew.

After a two-day jet lag decompression, we set the plan.

"Vanna, whatever we do, we need to do it all on one specific night. We'll never get their proverbial 'pants down' twice in a reasonable time frame."

"Unless they are drinking which they usually are."

"No, too chancy, and it's critical we remain incognito."

"The shear pin tactic will work on the 100 horse motors, but not on the trawler. Do you have something for that? Or would you prefer if I took the trawler myself?"

"Lance, how many times have I saved your life in the last three months? Do you know how to mount an underwater limpet mine, for remote control? Sometime when I am deep in my cups and of high spirit with Greg and Cheryl, I will convince you why you should have no stress for me. Now, I will have to make two trips, one alone to the trawler and one with you to the 100 horses."

"Ok, ok, we go on the first moonless night. We need to reconnoiter a few nights to locate a pattern."

"Lance, I will need the underwater transport. You wait for me with the electric. When I get back, we will go directly to cripple 100 horse bays. Things will remain quiet from our point, until my gifts on the trawler or the 100's pull out to rip and ruin."

"Take whatever we have that you need. I will bring the shear pins with an extra, if necessary. Be sure to pack a flashlight."

The moon was waning. We left at 1:00 a.m. three nights later. We could never be faulted for being too close, but we slept seriously tight those three nights. We also monitored the usual movements of the three craft.

We started from the dock in the rescue boat in normal gear. We had not informed Songbird, nor would we ever consider the straps the corrupted Congress had tied behind their backs. The new interrogator was still there.

We throttled down to and affixed the electric motor for the trip to four hundred yards off the trawler. As usual, it was moored on the seaward side of the huge cement block that once-upon-a-time had provided glee for the non-cartel kids. Nobody noticed aboard but Vanna waved my concern off and slipped into the salty water. She had a single lead weight that kept her mask above the waves when she wanted.

The heart-throbbing waiting time settled in for me. I put out two spear guns and sound-suppressed pistols in plastic zip-lock bags. In stress, I swayed forward and backward in the boat. Fantasizing what we had and what we might lose. I realized my short wave-length sways might carry to the shore. I froze and put on the remainder of my wet suit.

Without even a heavy breath, Vanna wiggled over the transom. I sighed in relief. We held a quick hand and she pushed me to the throttle. Her expression was combat mode. It was a "see, I've been here before look." Quiet as the night our electric carried us to the head of the bay.

"Lance, I heard some noise on the shore but nothing on the trawler. It could have come from the block where the 100's are docked. I'm not sure, but be super careful. Give me my titanium pin."

We cut the electric motor and anchored five hundred yards from our targets. We would need the submerged transporters until and unless we sensed a security presence. We disconnected and launched them quietly over the transom.

We slipped in pulled by the transporters. No extra lead weights necessary. No moon hovered over our mission.

We stopped at the prow of our respective target boats with the transporters silenced. We signaled that we had the tools and the pins. We slipped to the sterns of the boats where the motors were affixed, I to the starboard craft and she to the port.

As I lowered my face a second time toward the prop, my hood pushed a slight ripple to shore. All hell broke loose. I had the old shear pin removed, centering the "ringer". A shot rang out and I heard the splash inches from my head. I couldn't see Vanna, but she was surely head down. Another seriously ugly ragged bearded head came thundering out of the trees. He spotted Vanna and lined up to fire. Ducking a pending bullet, and firing, my spear went through his stomach, with not even a grunt. I fought to get my pistol out and the guy that shot at me was going to win the race. I ducked under wondering if I would be dying when I came up. The shot was again set off course by the water. I popped up to face the muzzle of his pistol. Right at me. A pfft sounded and he was in the water next to me, bleeding the red sea. I looked for Vanna. She raised herself above the side of the boat, small relieved smile, and finished the shear pin insertion.

We quickly met at the prow, affixed lines to a leg of each cartel radical and towed them out to the electric boat. We got in the boat and took a deep cleansing breath. Too soon!

The motors of three boats growled into operation. We had the moon on our side, but they had search lights. The trawler was cruising along trying to locate our camouflage. The 100's were darting about in every direction, outside the shrimp reef, disgusting oaths spewing. Over their roaring motors, our electric was invisible. We also couldn't hear each other. Twenty-five per cent of the shrimp bed was nestled between islands which faced the concrete pier where we had changed the shear pins.

Vanna urgently pointed, I understood, and headed feinting into the shrubs lining the island. Both 100's saw us. They ramped up to full throttle, engines whining, ragged beards brandishing smuggled American-made assault rifles. Heading directly into the shrimp reefs.

Side by side, within a second of each other, the propellers with the titanium pins ripped off bending one of the other two props. A second later, a flash, a screech, a ripping of metal and an explosion which hurt our ears. We ducked low. They hit shallow reef, the pins held, another propeller gave out bending a third. The drive shafts seized, flaming into pistons and cylinders. Housing spewed out of the back of the motors taking partial transoms with them. With the centrifugal force still pushing, two guys alive but bloody tried to glide their remainders out into the sea lane where the trawler patrolled to get picked up on their way to threaten shop keepers. The mangled parts of the 100's reached the lane, but the trawler ignored the drowning rag-heads. Such loyalty among cut-throats.

The 100's were down. The trawlers were leaving. Vanna, with iron determination pushed her first button. The prow submarined and they needed bailing. A limpet under the gas tank erupted starting an intense fire. Two singed black faces ran to douse the fire. The limpet under the pilot house decimated the center of the boat still above water. Three bodies of carnage. The pilot fell forward to the fore-deck free into the water, flailing, dragged under by his assault weapon and ammunition. The fourth limpet exploded. No chance, no remains to dispose of.

"Vanna, do you have anything else" The wreck is still floating. With a dark look, remembering what these people had done to Rayban and many families, she lifted her black box and triggered. The last limpet had been targeted for the front of the trawler.

We had made a lot of noise and now had to move quickly.

Three stops. Vanna drove and I jumped in where I was sure there was no armed opposition, which was nowhere. I pulled the Styrofoam float bars out of each of the boats that would normally keep them afloat. Not wanting to leave any evidence, I threw them to Vanna. We were at the 50-foot mark now, with the bonefish clouding the water rushing over the channel in the reef. The only evidence left was three bodies and blue-green gasoline on the surface. We attached them to the two others and headed to the four-hundred-foot depth two miles north. Vanna tossed a flare across the surface and the blue-green was yellow-gold and then none. We headed out with our muted engine.

We slept around the clock the next day not mentioning our mission to anyone. Our love and passion and stress and fear exploded. She made me feel much better. Her sounds said the same. Decent, selfless human life, survived from evil.

CHAPTER THIRTY

Subsurface Demolitions

Reclining in the Captain's chair one night, Rayban thought he heard an explosion well off shore in the direction of the Bay Islands. He relaxed again thinking that if there was a serious problem, he would pick up notice on the sea-band radio network. It was ten minutes later with no notice on the radio, two more explosions sounded. Nothing followed on radio, Octavio felt obligated as a concerned sea community member, to investigate and offer safety to any people in danger.

Nothing was shown by this point on radar, Octavio headed in the direction he estimated from his knowledge of the area. His crew assistant was home in bed. He fired the huge cruising engines not being able to add sail to speed. If asked, he would guess that the sound came from west of the Bay Islands. He headed between them. It was not a short journey but he could make it at 25 knots in less than two hours. The fog was like a scrim before the stage lights come up.

His radar was top of the line, but there was nothing pinging in any direction. On this night in this fog, there was no available technology that could help him. His gut instinct was that he was in the general area. He knew the bottom of most of the Southern Caribbean with a blindfold. He knew he was west of Guanaja and east of Roaban, the drug island. There was a huge undersea wall that dropped off to 150 feet and went straight down for an unknown distance. He was a scuba diver and had dived this wall to 130 feet which is sport diver limit. He had given himself another 15 feet below, but there was nothing.

Using all of the technology available, he dropped the "magnetic" fish finder. He knew it was accurate only to 90 feet, but what's to be lost. The boat on remote moved north to south above the steep drop-off. The wall moved mostly north and south, but as nature seldom agrees, there was occasionally a jog to the east or west. Actual depths were running at 150 feet. His finder indicated that. He had little hope. It had been a long day at sea and he was beginning to zone out, but suddenly saw what he thought might be the outline of a completely desiccated hull teetering at the edge of the wall. It was out of focus, with no bodies nor recognizable artifacts visible. It was not from Pirates of the Caribbean but he lost view of it as his boat moved under remote control. Maybe he was so tired he was imagining things.

He had heard no radio traffic. He put the boat on radar-driven cruise with no sail. There was no major reef nor obstacle between here and Sambo creek.

He reclined again in the Captain's chair with hope of a doze. According to his instruments, he had traveled a mile and a half when another explosion erupted.

By now, he had on record the latitude and longitude of the phantom boat. He programmed the target point and set the engines at full. He arrived in forty minutes, activated the fish finder, and cruised the wall from south to north. There were a couple of familiar looking rocks, but no sign of any boat. No sign of anything although it was at the edge of the wall and anything could have washed over that. Or maybe he had been hallucinating. He thought he saw a flash of red running lights to the north, but they disappeared quickly; he ignored them. As he pre-set the returning parameters, he thought he heard a small engine leaving the area to the north. He saw no running lights so decided to get home and get a good night's sleep.

CHAPTER THIRTY-TWO

Aboard Starr Resort Rescue Boat

"Vanna, I can see it on my underwater radar. There is another modern-rigged cruiser in the area. I have it on satellite radar. I have an idea who it is. He noticed the sunken trawler we put down but weather conditions forced him for home. I think it will fall off the cliff in a matter of a day or two. The shrimp piracy mustn't pay well with such a rusted trawler. Let's get behind the airport island, no lights and idle for a few minutes. Be careful of the weather. A northerner can bear down in twenty minutes. You may not even see it at night.

Resort crew, turn south-east and we'll meet at the dock. Go ahead and light your running lights. The new cruiser is pulling into Sambo Creek. My radar indicates there is no-one to see us.

We had a full group of divers and all Captains available. On the surface, all was smooth, but those who had been involved in security backup activities were waiting and wondering. I thanked and dismissed them and radioed to Roberto. He came for breakfast with wonder in his eyes. Off in the trees, Roberto said to Lance, "I have technology, too, and I know what you did for me. The bombs on the cruiser were obvious if you were listening for them. The 100's are also a danger and I didn't hear anything from there. I know I can't ask any more."

Lance quickly replied, "They're gone, but let's not discuss this any more for a long time."

It was like the Revolutionary war. We were using the tactics of the revolutionary fighters against a huge enemy. We hit and retreated to hide. We couldn't ever win against the drug lords and the country army in a direct fight. As inconspicuously as possible we had put the shrimp thieves out of business saving Roberto's future. The bombs weren't inconspicuous, but we had no craft to take that trawler out quietly. Clean-up left no evidence or clues. Any court case in an uncorrupt U.S. court would throw the charges out. We operated business as usual.

CHAPTER THIRTY-THREE

Back in the Nest, Lances Resort

As we relaxed from our first relief of the day, we settled into our emotional bubble.

Vanna, "Lance, this doesn't leave me with a great sense of joy. It does leave me with a much greater sense of security."

"Perhaps not joy, (you are where I find my joy), but I do agree with at least short-term security. I don't see any liability for Rayban. I am also proud of how brave our group faces these horrid, dangerous thugs. As fiercely as our spirits have fought, we have to keep focused on how they may be coming. We have the trip-wire fence and the surf alarm. I think we need to consider other options."

"I ordered the CCTV cameras and we can set them up after a day of rest and/or relaxation. They would be more dependable if a policeman or judge would even enter them as proof of anything against the Don J. Do Mondo. As much as it may represent the middle of the previous century, I think a dog, a big dog, could be a huge protection. Finally, for now, I think we need to keep a pistol or shotgun in our bungalow. Keep carrying the electric tazer in your purse, with pepper spray. I will continue to keep open channels with Songbird. I think I have protected them from any culpability with our responses. I should probably call them. Come over here, maybe a little bit later."

After we spelled "relief" again, we dozed and a strange bird call erupted outside our cabin.

"Don't come out. I don't need you to see my eyes."

Roberto off to catch a load of shrimp.

"Bye!"

The way he loped off down the hill, I think he had a real good time with Zulinda. I remembered hopping and skipping like that. Different girls. If ever, now was not the time to mention it to Vanna.

CHAPTER THIRTY-FOUR

Sambo Creek

A week and a half after the boiler explosion (limpet) event, we met again at Rayban's home. He had been doing some tours and four sports fisherman guides. The fish guiding was reaping thousands of dollars in an average month. The all-inclusive package was $500 per half day, $950 per full day. Ray knew intimately the fishing fields. Some his father had used. The fishermen always went home with satisfying catches.

Rayban said, "I have to thank you for dodging me and my cruiser in the (limpet) boiler explosion event. When I heard several explosions, I was tempted to go back in case you were in trouble. There could be other ears around so we referred to it as the 'boiler event'.

"No trouble, Octavio, we had you on radar while you were out. I didn't want you to be seen with us near the resort. We turned off our running lights. The weather helped and you didn't see us. We left well enough alone."

"Rayban, could we speak very privately for a minute?" He took us into the parlor he had renovated with some of the earnings. Don Felipe had been watching all improvements and maintenance carefully for maximum bribery or tax savings. He hadn't cleared the majority of the life insurance yet.

"Rayban, after the first boiler went down and your attacks continued, I realized that someone had to be informing the drug thugs of your shipments. The distances are too great with too much fog for them to guess and catch you out there. There is someone in Sambo Creek getting bribes for hurting you.

If a white-face like me is seen nosing around, the mole may be spooked. You're going to have to get support from close, definite friends. I suggest you use Zulinda's resort and breakwater as feints a few times until you can get scent of who is directly talking with the thugs. It's going to be a white-face drug connection because Don J. would never have any Afro-Latins working for him, other than golf caddies at illegal immigrants' slavery pay. Have your friends get it around town you are planning a long haul. I will get Zulinda's permission. I'm sure she will cooperate because we have lost some supplies by robbery at gun point. In fact, we are running some supply trips jointly with her boat captains. With arms. Rayban, you are going to decide what can be done with whoever you catch. There is no lawyer, nor judge that will punish or stop this. If you need support at that point, call me.

CHAPTER THIRTY-FIVE

Manatee Conservation Issues

All our night-time security activities went unknown to the client divers. Business was above average. And then came Bucky. He was a deep brown Chesapeake Bay retriever. He immediately warmed up to the resort guests. That was a problem. He was critical security and had to sound an alarm when a thug with a fire arm appeared. Roberto had sneaked him over to the resort. He had to come to take him back for more complicated training. Bucky needed some appropriately timed "mean".

CHAPTER THIRTY-SIX

Warning Attack on the Manatee Defense

Rayban served me a double Captain-coke. The conversation bothered him. Between the points of the small peninsula sheltering Sambo Creek outside of the breakwater and the first docks, lived a pod of Manatees. They don't move much, got very fat and were fun to watch. They eat sea grass and algae, are not carnivores. The non-cartel teen-agers sometimes play with them. Try to ride them. They roll over and dump them off. Tourists request them by name on the Bay tours.

Rayban Hernandez saw them every time he returned to his home inside the breakwater. Recently, he saw a dead one. They have no natural predators at these depths nor are they of any food or other value. Not a normal occurrence, he began to monitor the area.

Within a week, a canoe type-diesel-centered boat drifted to shore. Three older pirate stock teen-agers jumped out with tridents and set to jabbing them and worrying them, hurting them. Laughing and evil, interns for the next Mondo mafia Don J.

From his boat Octavio called them to stop. They ignored him. He set his throttles half forward, maximum wake and filled their boat with water. Cursing, they left only to return two days later. They saw Octavio coming and pulled their boat way up on shore. His waves had no effect. Octavio turned around and came out to our resort here to see if we had any suggestions.

We concocted a plan. Fewer would have to die this time, hopefully! The next time Octavio saw the young evil-doers,

Vanna, Roberto and I took our supply boat to an outcropping three hundred yards west of the manatee's nest. Bucky, our Chesapeake Bay retriever, stayed to guard the camp. Octavio went near their boat and warned them again to stop. With even more filthy language, they blew him off. He had his radio on so we could hear the invective. Octavio headed back toward Guanaja, the island of our resort. They had had their warning.

I put on the rest of my wet suit. At sundown, I would be invisible until I got very close. Staying under water, I moved to 15 yards away and shot the taller guy, who was gleefully stabbing, with my spear gun in his thigh above his knee. Warning, comeuppances! Unless I hit the artery, he would not be in mortal danger. They had cell phones so they got transport to the town hospital. An hour later, I checked with my hospital contact and the young punk had been treated and put on crutches.

Daddy pirate went screaming from bar to bar, helpless again because we had left no trail. Rayban had retraced his path coasting outside the breakwater headland. We waited another half hour, putted along to his boat, secured ourselves in the fish machinery, and headed in tandem at 28 knots back to the island. Only one discernable object. Only his running lights. Songbird's drone could have tracked us but they knew nothing of the conservation efforts that had gone down.

Our helpful contact with Songbird had been transferred to Costa Rica. His replacement was wedded to the rule book. He had been the one we had called when pirates were massing to invade the island and he said his ROE didn't permit him to intervene until they were actually on the island on private property. He was also the one who refused to interdict the Don J. Mondo because a later invasion fight was over and Songbird could not pick up a now non-combatant. Songbird was the one to call us a week after the conservation strike and ask us to come to his office. We chatted before we slept that night. Ray had not been called so we wouldn't mention him at all. A fishing expedition and we knew it. He knew it.

"I called. The meeting was at the military office. I wasn't treating anybody for lunch in this deal. Roberto, Vanna and I went. The atmosphere was ice in a climate of 95 degrees. I wasn't starting any conversation. The ball was in his court.

"I assume you know what we have to discuss here?"

I responded, "I do not."

"There was an assault on a young man out near the manatee nesting grounds late last week, Lance"

We looked at each other with steely feigned ignorance.

"What, they were assaulting the Manatees? A fisherman reported seeing a dead one floating there a couple of weeks ago."

Brainerd, you may refer to me as Mr. Starr and "I know nothing of that. We have been out on the island for two weeks now and today we are doing the usual supply run. We came over here first so we haven't heard any gossip. At this point since you ordered us here, I assume you plan to charge us with whatever it was."

"No, don't get ahead of yourself. I'm doing an investigation."

"Why out of the clear blue sky are we 'people of interest'? Somebody, maybe a drug thug, has something against us." I continued, "Wouldn't be the first time and based on no shred of reliable evidence."

"You have some evidence, some gut feeling we are secretly behind whatever happened? What did happen, inform us!

"Somebody shot a fishing spear through the leg of a young man."

"And why would someone do that?"

"We don't know why?"

"Were there any markings on any Manatee indicating human brutality?"

"We don't know. The local police were involved and didn't indicate anything."

"How many young men were involved?"

"Three."

"Any of their parents on the police force?"

"We don't think so."

"Do any of their parents have cartel businesses the police need to work with or purchase from?"

"Not that we know of."

"Then what in the name of incompetence leads you to suspect us. Ranger Brainerd, I am done doing your work for you. You are putting credibility on a club of cops who have their lips so glued to the drug cartel bosses that only major surgery could remove them. If you don't know that, the lawlessness rampant here on the north coast and islands is understandable. I have been here over six years. I have communications with a few people who speak to others and thus to everyone on the coast or islands. I know you haven't gone once into the American bar/restaurant. Nor to the best quality restaurant, nor to any dance festival, or concert.

"If you did that and had any awareness, you would know what this culture is, and is not. In that process you would learn that I and my associates involve ourselves only in self-defense from these thugs you are incompetently blind to. Hopelessly, we report any other theft or damage to our environment. Their bribe-driven police arrogantly ignore us. And now you question us?"

"You can be sure that every family in Sambo Creek knows we're here. Probably half of Cuenca. Some of them even know what happened. Those Manatees are part of their financial future. These young aspiring pirates will end up with much more hurt than a wounded leg if they continue. That's not a threat from me. You have a wider community to deal with, and at this time, good luck! You have no credibility!"

"Vanna and I are not married. There is no law involved forbidding testifying against husband or wife. Take her in the other room, ask what you need, and be done with it."

He came back flustered. Behind his back she had a devil smile.

I said, "Ok, this sham is over. I encourage you to choose your patsies more carefully next time. Very carefully or you will be unable to purchase any goods and services, other than from the cartel, from any store closer than San Pedro.

"Sorry, flight to SPS fully booked. Sorry, the bus is filled. Oh, we're out of fresh eggs. No sausages made today."

"You need to act to protect the community's financial future, not harass decent people trying to make a life in this drug-driven failed government. The only jurisdiction you have here is the good-will of the people. You need to recognize your enemies. In this region, you have many. Good afternoon."

Only that round of the desecration of the Manatees was over. It didn't end there.

These cartels are so inherently evil, they want to destroy even if it pays them little or nothing. Their poor little crooked teen-ager had an injury. The saga of the ghostly bone spur fisherman was entertaining the bar rooms of the entire north coast. A few knew. A few guessed in their beer. Every cop had a big enough bribe from Don J. to sweep the spur under the sand.

The ignorant and obsessed criminals considered it a point of honor. Their creativity beyond an attack of force was empty. The bars were full of the boasting and threatening. Juan and our Railroad Street communicators had us completely up to date.

Rayban pulled up to our pier on his way to Gulfport with flounders. We scanned his route with the resort drone and no criminal activity appeared. We checked the sea radar. Clear.

CHAPTER THIRTY-SEVEN

Continued Desecration of the Overweight Manatee: Impending Saga of the Errant Bone Spur

"Lance, Vanna, thank you for the notice of clear passage, but I am concerned again about the Manatee situation. These brainless vandals have gotten it into their head that the Manatees are the ones who have caused the problem. The vandalism of the young punks has been lauded by these fools. Juan Railroad says they have set a date to go out in force, a dozen or so fanatics, and destroy every Manatee and the nesting grounds. The department of natural resources is populated by the drug fool's friends, they know, and will plan to be on the other end of the country in the Mayan ruins during that week."

"Rayban, via my Railroad Street raga-muffins I've had that information since last Friday. We've been discussing what we might do to protect and create a legend that will continue to maintain that protection. We have a plan, but you will be integral to carrying it out. You have time to finish this delivery, but stop here on your way back and we'll finalize."

"To create the legend we want, this plan will need to include several synchronized parts. Unfortunately, to embolden its credibility, with this criminal population, there need be some fatalities. There will be no children included by these guys. Their manhood has already been called into question by the injury of their demon offspring. The skill level of the operations people and the bravery and survival attitudes of Sambo Creek will be strong enough to launch it."

"Rayban, in a status of reverse racism, you need to choose the darkest black volunteers from Sambo Creek. Darken their teeth. You need to meet those privately two or three times to coordinate the actions. Rayban, to give this some imagination and thus lasting relevance in the community bars for years, I will need to use a plane. We already know the department of natural resources is in collusion with this cartel desecration. From the Railroad Street kids, we know they will be in Copan at this time. I will be sending Roberto over there with Pedro Gonzalez and his two-seater Cessna. I will advance the costs of gas and pilot, but Rayban, I need you to speak with your association of tour groups to reimburse some when they can. Finally, Rayban, we need to run Sambo and Copan Ruins in tandem. For reasons you will learn later other things are in the mix. They need to be obvious that they are related. We will need you to evac. us to Guanaja from the area immediate after the action. Prepare to attach our boats as we did before.

Three days later, Vanna, two boat captains and I gathered five spear guns, one as a spare, and stationed two pistols in the gunwale of the security boat. Roberto went to Guanaja airport to fly to Copan. Rayban delayed, then launched from Sambo Creek break-water to amplify communication if necessary, and be ready to pick us up.

Actions by the thugs were reported to Bird-cage camp radio by Railroad Juan on a 15-minute basis. Rayban, in communication with the leader of the Sambo Creek group, his younger brother, got them immediately from me.

The beginning of the approach came as our Chevy engine settled from full throated glide toward a landing point 100 yards closer to the nests than the last time. I informed Rayban. His volunteers were on their own, except for emergency communication. They had heavy black tarp sacks to blind crooks and to avoid any recognition. The black forest attack group were cautioned not to speak or make any sound.

The boat captains, Vanna, and I in black face and black wetsuits swam below the surface toward the nest. A Manatee unhappy with our proximity rolled over away from us and under the bank. I raised my head to listen and could hear a few explosive cries and strikes in the dark forest.

I hurried us along. We needed to be at the main nest to stop any injury and combat the first marauders that might get through. We aligned ourselves, below the surface, parallel to each other facing the shore. Vanna and I had pistols in plastic bags at our waists should worst come to worst. This was not intended to be part of the plan but if things went south, the resulting plan could be the worst.

All hell broke loose as the first thug in the forest cried out and was muffled. He had seen nothing. Other cries and ensuing muffles continued. There were a dozen and a few got closer to the shore, but were still in the grasp of black phantoms stalking them.

We maintained our positions now with our masks breaking the surface. The plan was to wait and take out the first four that came to the nest. In the forest, back cloth bags were shoved over the heads of the white-faces already captured. Their rifles, pistols and ammunition were thrown into heavier gunny sacks. The darkest of the dark, so we couldn't make a site error, collect the sacks and dragged them over next to the boat.

The ruckus in the forest had quieted but we could hear tripping thumps of boots coming toward the shore. Four of them came bursting out of the brush with automatics at full bore. We were literally inches above the surface and suffered no casualties. There was no debate about defense versus offense. Without rising to a dangerous knee, we each put a spear in each midsection. They were immediately face down with their automatic's yards ahead of them in the sand.

I pulled my pistol, removing the plastic, and moved to stand up. I raised to fire when out of the brush came a phantom so dark, I could hardly see him in the shadows.

"Lance, stop, it's me, Ray's brother. Don't shoot."

"Ok, ok, relax, Octavio. Come and help the drivers' put hoods on these thugs and drag them to the boat."

Octavio Jr. raised up to come help and a crash came out of the forest on the west side of the nest. One step into the clearing, he was white. Then he was down, face buried in the sand, automatic two yards from my feet. He blindly reached for the American assault weapon. I was out of balance trying to bring my pistol to bore. I would never have time. Vanna did. One double tap. Love those damned Seals!

"Octavio, bag this guy and take him over to the boat. Reggie will be there with three more."

Vanna stepped over to me with a look of relief and love in her eyes. Our eyes met for three beats, then we jumped to get back to the boat and out of site.

The Drug-lord's bounty: the ones who would never be found. Rayban eased up next to us and our four extra-body-boat plus guns and ammo. We secured the two boats firmly and without any running lights, headed at 30 knots toward Guanaja. We headed a few hundred meters west of the island, then north for four miles and 200-foot depth. With hate, American guns and ammo, the thugs went to visit Davy Jones.

CHAPTER THIRTY-EIGHT

TV, Radio, and Social Media

Once more on Guanaja with the captains shooting strong relaxing liquids, I called Octavio Jr. for a field rep. Rayban, sitting next to me, was relieved to hear his brother's voice.

Octavio Jr, with relief in his voice said, "Those drug guys are down where your boat had been. The bags are still over their heads. They didn't see anything after we took them down in the jungle. We didn't have to kill any. We didn't speak so there is no voice to recognize. You have their guns and ammo. The fish are eating their clothes as they sit naked in the water at high tide on the beach. I think we should bind their wrists and ankles so we have plenty of time to disappear home. They'll get free in a few hours. Wonder what story they will be slurring in the bars tonight."

"Good idea, good leadership!" If anybody asks any of you anything, you know nothing of what happened tonight. Your families will confirm you were home in bed. To make a long-term aura of safety for the Manatees, there are other related operations in play now. When you hear them included in the legend someday, you can have fun embellishing and exaggerating the story. You will indirectly continue the safety for the Manatees. But you weren't there!

After checking with Octavio Jr, I contacted Roberto in Copan. The three jeep vehicles the department of resources drove out there had been pushed into the river overnight and their drive shafts and pistons were rusting. "There will be some surprised corrupt officials in the morning". In plastic in each vehicle was a message. "Saga of the Phantom Bone Spur, Confederate Version: 'The Manatees are a natural resource to the financial health of the North Coast. Your blatant attempt to collude with criminal elements and white supremacists to destroy them is known in every home. You may be liable to reaction from residents of the community. Your drug-controlled police will never be able to protect your disgusting actions from the thousands here who have a financial and emotional advantage from their presence. You are the brainless lackeys of the Don J.'s lords in this allegory. "

Finally, I called Juan of the Railroad Street regulars. "Do you have the sticky messages to put on the department of Natural Resources mail boxes and front doors?"

"Yes, half done, will be up by midnight."

"Can you get the other simpler forms in and around the bars?"

"They are already up. Generic pages on the bars, also."

CHAPTER THIRTY-NINE

Manatee Legend goes Viral

"Juan, can I talk to your sister about the Facebook and Zoom pages?"

"Yes, unknown person, she is right here."

"Yes, I'm here, Mr. Unknown person. But we hackers always find our person. We collect kisses in exchange. Facebook and Zoom are up. I also uploaded the form to Twitter, the code name there is #Lanna. Lance and Vanna, get it?"

Lance smiles, "Got it. Now, our major purpose here is to make this evening's actions into a saga, a legend of the invincibility of the Manatee. We want it talked about over beer on the north coast and islands. Even some publicity on the Panhandle might help. If there's an elementary teacher willing to include it in his/her fantasy curriculum, it would be great. Knowing a friend of a friend would work here. So, use your imagination. Every Manatee will have a kiss for your forehead."

Later the next day, Roberto returned to his island and Juan of the Railroad Irregulars reported the shock in the hungover crooks. Many who had not participated in the raid were recounting the myth with the greatest of embellishment. The Manatee saga had succeeded getting long lasting results.

CHAPTER FORTY

Second Run for Octavio

Octavio had announced a fish delivery trip and I was standing by at Zulinda's. This was a fake delivery trip that would go only as far as Zulinda's on the south of our island. Octavio's friends would be watching and Songbird and I would be monitoring by radar. Zulinda had quarters for Rayban for the night.

Vanna marched me right back to our cabin proving that the joy there, was more relief than any stirrings I might have popped from seeing Zulinda, Au natural.

CHAPTER FORTY-ONE

Just an Accidental Slip on the Trigger

Two weeks later a gas-powered boat came around the east end of airport island. Two men in Hawaiian shirts. We already had them on drone camera. Song-bird had checked in as well. They could have come from the Floating Suburb or the Drug Island. No black drone I could see. Bucky and Vanna with a Rueger ran down to what could be the landing point. Vanna held in the brush, but Bucky took down the first one that hit the beach. Vanna and I had seen no guns, so she told the one still standing to lay down right now. She got Bucky off the other; put him haunches down immediately. They were squealing. "We're from the Artificial Island, why are you attacking us? We can get a lawyer for assault."

"Yeah, you get a lawyer. You can get one from the mainland who will sell you right down the river to the drug cartel. Now let me see some identity. If you have any weapon, put it on the sand or your hand will be bleeding into the surf. The identity confirmed them as from the Island. I called Captain Brearly to confirm. Up on your knees. What are you doing over here at sundown?"

"We got bored and decided to have an adventure. "

"You have adventured onto a deadly no trespassing zone. You were one second from getting shot. There are two resorts on this island and if you want to set foot on either, get on the internet and buy a package tour. There is another island, Utila, west of here. It is mainly disgusting but you can visit. Now get your boat and get away. Where is that boat from?"

"We borrowed it from the animation office on the Neighborhood Island."

"I'll check that out. The last boat of this size came to attack and burn this resort. They were dispatched."

Looking up, shuddering, the 'adventurers' saw rifles with scopes focused on them from the nearest ramp boat, three on the path in the briars, one on the upper deck of the bar, a tripod on the tower.

"We are extremely sensitive. You are lucky!"

CHAPTER FORTY-TWO

The Sambo Traitor

In our emotional interlude we smiled certain how warm a welcome Rayban had received. Roberto was gone on the mainland getting Bucky advanced lessons. I rolled over face-to-face. Devine every time!

We had to do four more fake trips before Rayban's team located the traitor. Zulinda smilingly provided lodgings and breakfasts. Vanna kept me well entertained, under her finger (s), occasionally letting me go as far as the drone on our tower.

Rayban's culture was different from the others on the mainland. They had techniques that I was unaware of. However, the end result: the traitor was not seen again. We did another fake trip and there was no launch. Communication would be down for a while. Rayban said that remorse was an important element of their cultural response. The boy showed none. His family had no financial need.

A month of three trips north had no attacks. Octavio told me that another neighbor boy was seen on the sly with a thug. When the thug left, one of the mothers who had witnessed the event, took the boy and thrashed him severely and having his attention, explained the whole illegal situation. Octavio was an icon hero to the boy and realizing he could be putting him in danger, he broke down crying. None of this happened behind doors; this kind of information quietly, but quickly, spread throughout the community.

I was trying to decide a safe time to re-set my contracts in Germany, specifically in Frankfurt. With the setbacks we had dealt to the drug lords, I was anticipating another attack of some kind at any time. I stayed. I also pursued additional security. I had to pursue back-channels via Roberto. While Songbird had been supportive beyond their mandate, it couldn't continue to be expanded. I knew of trouble from a Senator from the south confidently pocketing "campaign donations" in Lempiras, currency of the 'Lords". His whole party would have to be voted out of office before I could be safe. I needed that technology of back-up and now, I needed it from Germany.

It was dangerous to pursue this in the corrupt business 'failed gun control' and government atmosphere in the U.S. This train wreck president was surrounded by ass lickers that could directly hurt my career, future, and life.

I contacted Greg in Munich on encrypted technology media. No hackers had developed ways of beating that yet. Within 24 hours, Greg had located the drone system I would need along with the apps that evolved it from defensive to pro-active. It would come via Roberto temporarily in San Pedro Sula. He could access it from cargo since veterinarian Alicia wasn't closely monitored by the cartel. Bucky was completing his training. He would transport it hidden in the shrimp boat which would be bringing Bucky back. With help from Carl from banana research I should have it up by the weekend.

Up on our island tower with alarmingly powered green lasers, we tried another 'feint' fish run to Gulfport. Rayban stopped and hid with Zulinda. Once again, I was removed by Vanna from Uncladbeach.com and thrashed into rapture in our little cabin.

As I was caressing her, I reflected that a little jealousy was providing some hot results. She was now leaning down very close, firm pinky to chest and using me to send her off to shriek-land. This position giving her control of my chest, and, well, my triumph, was taking us together into ecstasy.

Two hours before sunrise, I checked radar for any launch from Drug Island. Rayban had used another source to plant a fake trip. As he calculated, the false information got to Don J. Mondo. I launched my drone and targeted its infrared. We located the wake. I called Songbird.

"Songbird, this is aerial Birdcage. We have a wake leaving Drug Island in the direction Rayban usually takes. They will find nothing tonight as Ray is being hosted by Zulinda. I don't want to interrupt any of his activities, so could you confirm the Drug Island launch, over? I will power down and switch to land based radar. I'll maintain ground radar monitor until two hours before sunrise. Perhaps we could meet for dinner again and delineate ways to keep us from interrupting each other or running into each other. Over."

"Laudable, you're keeping Rayban's engines from cooling. I suspect Zulinda makes you redundant. Congress is cuckolding so many sycophants, our activities should be lost in the corrupt ether."

"Birdcage, we'll be glad to have lunch. Don't worry about any in-sky collision. Military grade drones fly up to 10,000 feet, way beyond what your bird could access. We could review "defensive maneuvers" which we have unofficially monitored before. Frankly, after the destruction wracked by the 'Unknown Islands Revenge' person or group, we anticipate terror at any time. If you feel you are a target, harden your defenses soon. Out."

"We've got tripwire, surface alarm, CCTV, Drone defense and offense, and Bucky. We are low on assault weapons which we know they use. We need two more noise-suppressed rifles, 300 Weatherby. We may store but avoid using RPG and hand-grenades. We should at least mention the situation to Zulinda. Out."

"Starr group, go to camp radio."

"Vanna, could you dress, or undress as needed and go over this with Zulinda?" I don't want to come back hog-tied by you tonight. I have to set the drone for monitoring radar if our ground unit powers down."

"Roberto, could you get the rifles and ammunition, both regular and tracer. One set of infra-red goggles would be good, too, although we have it on two of our sniper rifles."

"Ladies and gentlemen, this assault of theirs will start either early morning, or late evening. What they are preparing bodes an attack in two or three days. They will be forced to come by boat and will want to use sunrise or sunset to camouflage their movements. Keep them off shore for as long as possible. Start with rifles with regular ammo. Second clip should be tracers. Don't doubt for a second, they are here to kill us. You cannot hesitate." If they have a new Don J. Mondo, take him out immediately. There is no iota of a chance anyone will take him to trial."

"I will go down and see what the boat captains are willing or able to do."

I had been dreaming of some draught German beer and providing some lovely carved ceilings for Vanna to ponder as I was pondering her. But I was feeling it in the breeze and in my bones. The destructive forces were forming. Railroad Juan was restive, anticipating. I had not taken any dive groups for that month.

CHAPTER FORTY-THREE

Major Attack, Vanna Hurt

Roberto, Vanna and I had agreed that if this raid took place, and if we survived, we needed to take the fighting to them. Roberto had bought the shrimp fields and in closing received maps of all the lot lines on the island including the large fort. I flew the drone over at altitude and located the room large enough to hold armaments and ammunition.

Vanna said, "We are dealing with a large group of greedy bastards, and we can't go in there and expect with our small numbers we can neutralize them. I can devise explosive charges that will equalize our chances. These should combine with what they have in there and bring that part of the castle down. The drone is powerful enough to take what we need in two trips. If the time comes and we see them moving our way to attack, we send the first drone load as they are leaving the shore. Lance, I assume you can deliver the load right on target. The second load must go immediately so you can get the drone back to support the battle.

Songbird had sensed it first. Bucky began growling patrolling the beaches. Roberto, this time, had been jogging in place, so to speak, at Zulinda's. I called him back and told her to prepare whatever she had. Rayban was heading home for the evening after collecting "$2000" for the day. He reversed at full plane. Distances involved put him in Zulinda's cove with minutes to spare. I went down and recruited the boat captains. They got suppressed-fire rifles from the boats. They had been wearing pistols on their belts for a week now.

I went through the thickets and thorns to the top of the hill between the resorts. I sent the drone to surveil. Songbird had called the beginning. They came back concerned that there were seven boats coming mostly manned by three crooks apiece. My drone called five boats headed for the dive resort and two toward Zulinda. Vanna was on the ridge of the hill to the west. Roberto was at the veranda at the top of the resort. I informed Vanna and asked her to forward the information to Zulinda.

"Songbird, they are definitely on their way. Can you begin support? Over."

"Birdcage, staffing change, we can't respond until we confirm they are actually feet down on the island. Over".

"Songbird that will be too little, too late. Turn away. Look somewhere else. Go hunt forest fires or something in the mountains. Brainerd continued to be a pw congress sucker. The guy we needed was in Costa Rica.

I focused the laser green and demolished the gas tank on the first skiff. No noted survivors.

Bucky stormed along his usual patrol path then disappeared in the quickly gathering darkness.

"Rayban, are you in position?"

"I'm anchored at Unclad, all guns on deck."

"Rayban, if you're alone, urgent you repel boarders. Hold for me! I am waiting until the second skiff is 30 meters from shore. Drone is set to green. I will focus on gas tanks. Upon the first detonation, fire at will, fire for effect."

"Zulinda, they will be visible coming around the point in three minutes. Still two boats and six marauders. I will fire at their controls and tank. Within 45 seconds Rayban will strafe your beach. Get behind your bunker on the west end. Get the others down. If I'm late, start 300 magnum rifle fire. Rayban, immediate support!"

The first invaders were decimated by the boat captains. Roberto hit three from the veranda. Then a flash out of the dark, Bucky went for the throat of the first invader staggering from the burning boat. A scream but the crook was still alive, losing blood. He turned to bring fire on Bucky, was blown backwards by a shot from above. From 100 yards. And died. Vanna turned away.

I joined Roberto and the captains to finish off the five remaining crooks, late off their boats.

"Vanna, sitrep on Zulinda?"

"Some of the crooks have made it to her beach. Rayban has them in a brutal cross fire but there are places to hide. You may need to calm Octavio, he's panicking with every bullet sent to protect Zulinda."

Reluctantly, surprised I had to correct my Seal. "Vanna, this is not the time to calm Rayban. I'll get to him when it's not so dangerous."

Lance To Zulinda, "Zulinda, Vanna is on the briar path. How can she help?"

"Lance, I need her. My clients were warned and are dressed appropriately, two with pistols. That is far from enough."

Zulinda to Vanna, "Vanna, Lance says you are in position. My clients are not dressed. Please move quickly to the small house on the right side of the beach. Vanna, get rid of all your vestments. Fire on anybody who is dressed."

Lance, "Rayban, continue to cover Zulinda and look for marauders with any kind of clothes on. "

"Roberto, Bucky has another late-comer in his sites. Back him up, quickly. I think there are two crooks that have gotten into the trees behind you. Send Bucky out there!

"Rayban, sitrep on Zulinda?"

"All clothed people are dead or debilitated on the beach. Nude ones including Vanna and Zulinda are walking around checking for any dropped firearms. "

Lance to Songbird, "Only one repairable injury. The Don J. Do Mondo is making an escape right now across the airport channel. Now that he has attacked us, can you finally do something? Over."

"Birdcage, our ROE does not permit us to interdict fighters in flight. Sorry, over."

"Who the hell is writing your ROE, Cruze?

"Songbird, turn your congressional corruption-driven drone and your heads away from the field of battle. For the meagerness of your help, you better go again and check the mountains for fires."

"Rayban, strike your sodium gas floodlights and start a recon trip along Zulinda's beach continuing promptly around airport channel and along to our dive pier shore. We need to be sure we have no loiterers lurking with arms. Protect yourself, I think there may be two up in the forests near the path between resorts."

"Roger that."

He made the oval turn around the point and a bullet pinged off his windshield. He looked up the hill and Bucky was wrestling the neck away from the brute who had fired. Roberto in the woods fired and the crook stilled, death rattle audibles through the forest. Then from behind him, Roberto was under fire. He dived to the ground unable to see the shooter. He jumped toward uncladbeach.com and a thicker tree. A bullet missed his ear by a finger. He was wondering if this was going to be the time and the place. He heard a rustle in the thorns and tried to turn. A suppressed 'thwang' bullet went out over his head. Still alive, he looked up the hill and a crook fell sideways from behind a tree, gun-in-hand. Then he didn't. Roberto looked behind thinking he had been hit and was in heaven. Vanna, completely in naked camouflage, lowered her gun and reached to help him up. She scoured and hunted for any scratches on Bucky.

Roberto went on and Vanna went back to Zulinda's. She strode over to the little shack she had cleared earlier. She recovered a knapsack.

Vanna, on camp radio not connected to Songbird, "Lance, where is our target? We can't lose this despicable Don J.? Songbird will not help."

"Vanna, wait 60 seconds. Our ROE is "survival". She hit the button at 58.

The drone ordinance put Don J. Mondo directly under the concrete column of the armory. What was left of him looked similar to Bucky's droppings. The drone came back to me for re-armament. If any, there would be limited communication with Songbird. Somewhere I couldn't locate, there was a Senator "on the take." You could get two lempiras for a dollar, so it was worth the subterfuge.

CHAPTER FORTY-FOUR

Vanna's Wounded!

Roberto, in the blur of Vanna's beauty, had seen some blood on her shoulder and back. He followed her to Zulinda's beach and saw her set off the armory explosion. Bye, Donny J!

Roberto: "Vanna, you're injured! Lance, Vanna is bleeding in two places, not heavily but Rayban, can you bring the first aid kit. Vanna. Sit down!

In the background of Roberto's radio call I heard her chewing him out for bothering. "It's no big deal!"

I agreed with Roberto, Vanna bleeding was a big deal. I grabbed the remote drone control and flew through trees and barbs. When I got there, the screen showed Zulinda gently lowering Vanna's glorious front face down on a towel. Rayban was coasting up on the sand jumping off with the military first aid kit.

Zulinda assertively said, "I've got this Lance, float down, relax. Vanna, lay still. Rayban, give me the local anesthetic, antibiotic and the butterfly Band-Aids. Vanna, this will hurt for a few seconds until I get the local anesthetic applied. Vanna was still tense even after the cream was in place. She could see my face hovering by her side when she turned her neck to her left. I was watching my facial expression on the drone screen or she could see my worry. There was a three-inch laceration on the upper left side of her back. I could see it was not deep, but I struggled to hide my worry about the amount of blood. Perhaps the butterfly Band-Aids, several, would keep it together. Zulinda cleaned the wound; applied the antibiotic. Girls knowing girls, she told Vanna that it would heal with no scar. Vanna was still tense.

I looked and on the towel in two places there were more splotches of blood. We would have to get at the injuries but now couldn't have her lay on her back. Zulinda gently helped her to sit up on the log. On her left shoulder and for an inch under her arm, was another laceration, this one also not too deep. Three regular Band-Aids and antibiotic would serve. Hidden under the fold of her left breast was another instance of blood. Zulinda gently raised the nipple so she could see. At first glance it looked like the entrance wound of a bullet. We had to ask.

Vanna said, "I thought so, too, but I sensed and applied pressure. I felt no metal in the wound. As I was stripping and running to the beach, I tripped on a log and fell flat on my face. I think my uncovered breast hit on a piece of shale which temporarily embedded itself in the wound. When I jumped up to start running again, it dropped off."

The wound was not deep, but Zulinda cleaned it carefully and applied some antibiotic. Again, she specified, "No Scar." However, we were out of butterfly Band-Aids. A minute later, Mickey Mouse was peering out from under her breast. She couldn't see that and nobody was in the mood of laughing out-loud. We had the distasteful task of removing and hiding 13 bodies.

Bucky was sure of all the locations so we affixed them on 13 ropes to the transom rail of Ray's boat. We towed them to avoid getting any blood on his deck. Critical: leave no evidence. Went out to the 150+ foot depths, wired rifles and American pistols to their owners, and committed them to Davy Jones locker. Finally, we policed both resorts for incriminating evidence.

We sent Rayban back to his work. He now kept the rifles in his boat. I ministered faithfully to Vanna's wounds, certainly more pleasure for me than for her. Finally, she pushed me on my back, and in my view, Mickey Mouse was no longer there.

CHAPTER FORTY-FIVE

The Meshkitia, Floating Island Suburb

We took a four-day run down to Trujillo at the east end of the country and a few miles north of the Meshkitia province. The Meshkitia is essentially a swamp. Some gringos set out to fish there but were driven back by mosquitos. Some unusual primitive art comes out of there being sold in the bigger town on the north coast.

The reason to go to Trujillo is the healing of wide white sand beaches and the mild winds coming in off the Atlantic. Specifically, it is the place for a novice wind surfer to develop his or her skills. I grew too tall too late and balance has never been my strong suite, even on water skis. I had purchased a surfer which I learned the hard way was too long and heavy for me. I took it out and fought to keep my balance and let the wind carry me along. Vanna in her typical Uncladbeach.com bikini lounged on the shore chuckling. She was in an unspoken, continuous competition with Zulinda who would be around, but not often. Too much trying to get up, I concluded it was the wrong surfer for me. I took it over and put up with the constructive criticism with laughter from Vanna.

"Ok, you go and see if you can do any better." She pulled it over to the surf line, standing up already, moved it out two meters so the balance fin under the board was off the bottom, jumped up, settled the boom for her height, and went out for thirty minutes never falling. She didn't grow too fast for her balance.

"Your scuba, handle boats, blow them up, nurse, and are a crack shot. Where did you learn to wind surf?"

"Right here. I watched what you were doing and realized the changes needed, picked them up along your way. Changed them."

We went back to the lightly populated hotel and I demonstrated some of the skills I had picked up along the way. Any amount of noise was ignored by the guests and thrilled at by me.

We wandered over to the stand-alone local's restaurant "shack". It was one of those that look not too good, but the food is a knock-out. We sat outside on the beach chair and added a cold Salva Vida beer.

All day we had been concentrating on the wind, the sail, and the surf. We succeeded in repressing our cartel worries. At the restaurant our eyes wandered further around. There was a narrow channel at the end of the peninsula. Something out of alien comic book rumbled in. Off to the right of that channel was a small island or homestead. Walking around for a different perspective, we found huge metal ramps stowed above surf line. We went back to the chef of our restaurant who gave us the full explanation.

It was technically an island, but one the size of a good size suburban neighborhood. The chef said the captain of the moving behemoth had stopped in for meals a few times asking questions about where he could moor his monster and have a mooring that could support a bridge so residents could drive their cars off for day trips, shopping, or tours. The people in the Mesqitia province had voted down the idea of having it parked there. The chef knew about the Starr Dive Resort and he knew of the Bay Islands as well. He also knew well the inroads the drug cartels had built there. I asked if he had a phone number from the "island". He did.

Vanna and I went back to the beach chairs in front of our hotel. She still had that Unclad.com bikini. With the excuse of an evening wind coming in cold, I hurriedly escorted her into the room and back up against the door. She kissed me hungrily and eased herself right down. There are some very alluring activities that can be done from this position, but I carried her still joined back to the bed. She stayed on top, used me according to her desires. I was happy to be the "boy toy. Her wounds were healing nicely. I could now get myself back to lucidity and talk about what I had pondered.

We lay observing the rustic ceiling with the fan washing over us. It was that temporary time bubble when inhibitions fade and we give voice to emotions and seldom spoken dreams, sometimes a gentle kiss or two. Always the truth. We have to watch the energy buildup of these kisses or experience a double-bubble.

"Vanna, that's the first time I saw that island. I had read about it and Roberto mentioned something about it in passing. I didn't internalize anything about it until I saw it today. I got the phone number and think we should call the captain, introduce ourselves and get together and welcome them to the country.

Vanna muses, "Fine with me, but that wind surfing wore me out. Come over and wrap me up."

CHAPTER FORTY-SIX

Floating Suburbia

I got on the internet and found several such populated mobile, islands, many in Asia, at least two in the Caribbean; some being built in The Netherlands.

I called and introduced us and the resort. The captain sounded bored and was happy to invite us to lunch. We walked over the metal bridges and a sailor guided us six blocks into the neighborhood where the wheel houses, captain's dining room and his bedroom were located. He was in a beach chair in the shade of the bridge. He was, except for a pipe, the mountain of a man you would welcome to be your captain. He was a no-nonsense guy with a large round face on six feet five-inch body. Huge hands with rough, sea-claimed skin; receding hairline but always a mariner' cap. He was piloting not a ship but a neighborhood for a large corporation so his dress was crisp and proper. The eyes could give him away. The black pupils could go grey and sparkle if the situation was humorous. Solid black and glaring if things were going wrong. Vanna immediately brought the sparkle.

Although the resort was 1/30th the size of the "neighborhood", we were both captains with similar responsibilities. Lots to share. One important part of that was the drug spider legs crawling most places. The other was where the neighborhood could come to rest, for a long time. I described the possible location where a mooring could be renovated for vehicle traffic on and off. The main drug Island, Roaban had a runway long enough for big jets. People who could afford to have a home on this seaworthy land mass could easily have at least a small private jet, or a big one. The north shore was wide enough for several mooring/ bridges. There were some decent restaurants on the Drug Island, but heavily under the thumb of the drug lords. A very short plane hop or catamaran to the mainland offered other bars and eateries. The Copan ruins were a comfortable one night overnight stay away.

I met with Roberto who owned the shrimp farm and whose father had some contacts in the government and made the introductions for Captain Brearly.

There was the expected 'bar fight' from the drug cartels. The bottom line was that the "island" would have to pay inordinate taxes, clearly obvious bribes. The next to bottom line was that this world-huge corporation was of a higher stance than even a joint group of cartels could threaten. With their own renowned lawyers and aggressive security, the taxes were brought into line. Felipe, Rayban's lawyer, hidden in the background, gave valuable consultation on the state of the failing government. There was animus in the cartels.

Upon the 'Artificial Island's slow, inertia-controlled arrival at the drug island, Vanna and I invited the captain for dinner at the resort. I had spoken with him several times as the legal wrangling went on. We had met for drinks and dinner in the bigger town of Cuenca. Now he would see the resort and get an earful of the brutal attacks and blockage we and other businesses had been experiencing. From him we did not hide much, including size of decimated forces. We also highlighted the huge building/fort he would be moored nearby. It was the pimp-Lago of the high Don J. Do Mondo. Brealy listened, not showing much concern. We would soon learn why.

One pleasant side of the dinner was the surprise that a lovely young lady, darkly tanned, from the region, hopped out of their arrival boat. It's pretty clear that many of the big boned conquistadores had inserted some of their DNA into the population. The hair had remained black, but thick and shiny. The eyes also were brown, but with golden speckles that communicated mirth. The obvious trait surviving was the presentation of the breasts. Norwegian for sure. Long legs and excellent command of English: Maria Fernando Cardenas Brearly.

Three weeks after the arrival and mooring, all the rich and famous friends and family of the island dwellers flew in and attended a monumental gala dinner and dance. Dressed to the nines, the humidity soon corrected that mistake, but there was powerful A/C in the essential places. Planes arrived Friday and Saturday freshening up/some snorkeling hosted by Vanna and I, and the ball Saturday night. People slept in on Sunday, guests leaving in the afternoon. Planes jockeying for line up on the tarmac gone by 6 p.m.

Monday morning the first bomb went off on the ramp leading to shore. The captain called me to consult. Against my better judgement, he decided to brush it off and ignore. The bomb was not professional nor very damaging, quickly repaired. The following Sunday late morning, the second bomb went off leaving a scratch on the heavy boiler plate on the front hull near the water. The captain's wife, Maria, called and urged us to avoid using our drone on Thursday night. No explanation.

CHAPTER FORTY-SEVEN

The Explanation: Black Uniformed Swat

We did use our drone to surveil Black Bird Tuesday and Wednesday. We saw his black drone above us watching, watching. We powered down when we went to bed Thursday. Bucky was on alert doing his rounds. At three in the morning, we heard the thump, thump of helicopter rotors. Vanna, always alert, waked me. We hurried up to our veranda on the top of the resort with binoculars. On the castle, East and West side, were two helicopters; guys with black clothes and helmets. They went inside the Don J's Mondo fort/brothel; we no longer could see other than a shape occasionally. We began to hear explosions which flashed out the windows. They traveled around the decks and gun shots rang out. A moment later, six of the SWAT types stepped out of a door of the east side of the fort. It was no longer time for a flash-bang. Two heavy metal grenades into the room.

Vanna narrated play by play of this causing me to wonder again about her past. No more rifle fire from there. On the distant side of the now decimated structure, two more shots were heard. Two double taps responded. Some barked orders and yelling civilian-style rang across the water. The SWAT people boarded the helicopters and left. My airport sea radio had registered no request to land nor take off. Bucky had been leaping around barking excitedly; he couldn't control himself. He couldn't tell if SWAT was friend or foe.

Speculating, we went back to bed. Actually, Vanna knew, wasn't speculating at all. Bucky had to sleep with us.

CHAPTER FORTY-EIGHT

The Clean-Up and Deadly Warning

At 6:30 a.m., Maria called again and woke us up.

"We are sending a boat for you. Would you please come over now? You heard the noise last night."

I looked down at our dock and Captain Brearly was on their security boat with one other armed "Island security" guy. I waved and hurried down, first asking if Vanna wanted to go.

She wanted to sleep in, "been there, done that. I know what happened. Two much interruption last night."

Brearly didn't want to talk much at all in the boat. We went immediately up to the bridge. We found three security guards, and two pirates. One was the Don J. Mondo. He was obvious of mouth and dress. Huge khaki shorts on a bigger butt.

The captain addressed the lackey.

"You have a chance to live tonight, maybe longer if you take me seriously. You go back to whatever Davy Jones candidate is out-ranking Don J. Mondo here, and inform him of everything that happened tonight. Tell him I can call that in at any point I feel it is necessary. If I should be hurt or killed, there are two other officers who will do the exact same thing. He may have a billion-dollar illegal drug business, but he has locked horns with a trillion-dollar real estate business. This group of nameless-faceless owners will literally crush anyone interfering with its success. If you are ever seen in this area again, we will assume you are an enemy combatant. I recommend you go to the mainland

and get a legal job."

At that, Don J. Mondo blurted out, "You will not do that. If you persist in this, I will bring down such a fantastic, fantastic force of attack, if you live you will have nightmares for the rest of your life."

Brearly dangerously growled, "If you leave here, you will bring back "Hell's Attack. Is that right, real fantastic, and I quote you, fantastic destruction?"

"That is fucking right. You will not know where nor when it is coming."

"Will you be coming with it?"

"I will be fucking leading it."

"Probably a thinking man should try to mitigate effect of that attack early on. I can immediately reduce the coming leadership by one."

Brearly turned so Mondo was in front of his lackey. He brought his pistol up, black in his eyes, and shot him in the head, the blood and bones splattering the lackey.

Looking at the lackey, the captain said, "You can tell your 'sleeping Donny J., or whatever, that, too."

He nonchalantly walked back into his office. We ignored the janitors cleaning up the mess. He asked me a few details about my counter attacks, offered coffee. Maria brought the coffee and stayed. There was a lot more here than a coffee server or North Coast Bed Warmer. Later, I informed Vanna.

They both walked me back down to the security boat. Maria got on the boat next to the driver. She had a 300 Weatherby on her hip.

I waited to leave for Germany for two weeks. No peeps from anywhere. I would be relaxed in Frankfurt. There was a new sheriff in town.

CHAPTER FORTY-NINE

Germany, Another Reprise

We flew vagabond's choice, visited the airports of New York, Toronto, Ireland and Munich before landing in Frankfurt. Thank goodness for free airline drinks. Vanna wouldn't ask that again. By the time I had the pleasure of seeing her complete Venus, both the wounds under her breast and under her arm were pink traces. The deeper one on her arm was still red, but not infected red. We called Greg and alerted him we were in-country and would come to see them someday.

Vanna remembered her large shopping venues. In one month, I had four serious Mercedes concentration evenings. Any wounds were long forgotten although we didn't move from the room, mostly the bed, for four complete days in the new time zone.

CHAPTER FIFTY

Vanna's Mysterious History

After that heavy month, we ran down to Munich to catch up with Greg and Cheryl. Friday night heavy with beer and pork, we brought them up to date.

I had forgotten to have the big conversation with Vanna about the experiences or training that led her to be so multi-talented. I thought it might be nice for Greg and Cheryl to know. They were my family here and Vanna and I were seriously sweet on each other. The conversation started, as always, with limited answers to general questions.

I complained. She relented.

"After boot camp, and serving four years in the Navy, I got an undergraduate degree on the VA plan in Biology with Anatomy as the required minor. I got the license as a Nurse's Assistant. For eight months I worked in the medical ward on a large battleship. Absences and illness on the part of some doctors required me to perform duties above my normal training with grueling, sometimes panic-stricken hours of over-time.

"I registered to enter medical school, but could not face another five years of theory. From my experience aboard ship, I realized the rank and file treated doctors as their pawns. Without any choices given, they were sent around the world. Their life was arbitrarily limited by the next echelon of administration. I had intense training and experience but didn't want that external control."

"Application to the Navy Seals became available to women. I was accepted into a new more demanding form of boot camp. I faced the harsh treatment women were getting for entering a field that had been only male. I fought back and pushed over any obstacles put in my way. Of a group of 100 candidates, I was one of four selected. I joined a group of five men and specialized training ensued. I trained in scuba and extensively in both land and under-water demolitions. I labored on the pistol range. I joined in several dangerous overseas missions. Part of the training was in the new technology of drone warfare. Having played computer games incessantly, I enjoyed and surpassed minimum capabilities. Advanced knowledge of jeep and car repair is required of every Seal. I served four years, but although beholden for my training, I burned out on the death and destruction. I can't get away from it completely, but here I personally see the evil."

"I came to Central America with a Scuba Club, met Lance; here I am. Does that that answer your questions? Oh, I also trained on small and marine engines, gas and diesel."

"Wow, Vanna that is amazing. I can work more effectively and safely with you."

Vanna retorts, "As of now, Lance, you're not under-using me. I have some uncomfortable thoughts about removing those thugs, but from what I see of their savagery, there is not a correctional facility that could touch them. Even if there were an actual legal system."

"We should head home?" All computer script for Mercedes apps up to date and employees re-trained, we headed back to the warmth of Central America.

Compared to the third-grade teacher from the Frankfurt base elementary school, Vanna was frivolous in returning. Roberto had been in the usual bi-weekly skype contact and things were better than ever to see.

CHAPTER FIFTY-ONE

Caribbean Return

The captain of the "Island" became a good neighbor. His wife, Maria, didn't dress as risqué as Zulinda so Vanna was quick to warm up to her. I reflected for a moment on the strikingly beautiful women associated with Greg, Roberto, Me, and Brearly. They were breath-taking. We were definitely above middle class in finances. Are we unknowingly living the decadent lives of congress and the president's temporary trophy wives? Those interludes with Vanna debunk anything we might think of her, compared to the president's present trophy. Ours have advanced degrees in difficult fields. No, we're well above that swamp, now desecrated to a chess pool.

Brearly did take an unreported walk over to Unclad.com to meet the owner and establish amiable relations. Maria got a big surprise when he returned.

Roberto had increased dive groups, which certainly was good. There were still some snipping aggressive irritating actions from the cartel who hadn't replaced Alicia's father-I-law, deceased menace. Brearly brought me up to date. A bomb was placed in the water offshore of my beach on the airport side of the resort. No damage, it could have destroyed my future in one fell swoop. I went livid to Brearly. He said, "We're having some problems as well. We cleaned out that fort when you were here before. The problem is centered in the large apartment block south of it. Give me a night to ponder and get some home-office feedback."

I returned to the resort and surveyed all the intruder devices. I even checked Bucky's health. Having a protection device out in the water 30 meters from shore or pier was not feasible.

Vanna was bright and recovered from jet lag. I told her about the problem and that I had shared with Brearly. She wasn't letting anything dampen her returning spirits. "Fine, Lance, you've done what you can tonight. We'll get some news from the captain tomorrow. If you need to worry about it, you can start then. Let's go up to the veranda, share a champagne, and celebrate my shopping. I have some things for you that we may need to open later.

The things she got for me were really for her to wear. She'd have them on for 20 seconds.

The things for me were underwear more suited for German winter. Some pieces were designed not to block my frequent targeting exits. These would not hinder her access to whatever she wanted. A little champagne and frivolous enjoyment of anything in a bed where we sleep unclothed. I found her and she found me and I forgot all about the drug thugs.

The captain called and requested we meet in my cabana. Vanna was there and listened in. The corporation had added up cost of vandalism repair. It crossed their limits by too much and they said either he would fix it or they would. That is not really a "choice" statement so he told me to take down my drone again at midnight, Wednesday. He said he had many pieces of Intel tracing the repeated damage to that block building. The building was only thirty yards from Roberto's shrimp offices.

CHAPTER FIFTY-TWO

Black Security Returns

Vanna and I had several love meetings during the days in advance. In our relaxed emotional bubble after joy, we discussed the ramifications of the impending defense response. As much as I respected her concern for people, I had seen too much lawless damage done by these radicalized thugs, whole families' frequently. Without any uncorrupted legal system, there was no intermediate method to stymie this.

We put the drone down at bed-time and wrapped each other up to try to sleep and avoid the blasts that would surely ensue. We put Bucky directly into bed with us.

I went over the next morning to see what needed be done. Vanna didn't want to go. Somberly Brearly said, "Lance, It's a disaster. The building was full of armed resistance. Rocket propelled grenades, 55 mm machine guns, and bullet proof vests. They are gone and our SWAT cleaned up somewhat but we need your ramp dive boats to transport the remainders."

I called both boat captains and with the help of a dozen security guards, we weighted and sent the bodies out to the 200+ feet hole, this time a mile west of the previous. It was not discussed again.

CHAPTER FIFTY-THREE

R&R

The remainder of the winter season was the finest we had had in several years. The drug thugs had lost a great number of their attack boats and personnel, as well. The "Island Captain" had sent some gruesome messages about bothering his clientele. The bloodbath of the apartment block was one, and sent a shock through the community. Some cheered, but many were disappointed that their country had become so lawless that these revenges were the only push-back to crime.

We garaged the drone; the Artificial Island had their own to share if needed. I locked up the pistols and rifles leaving one rifle to each captain. Rayban had gone to Trumpland and traded a Weatherby for an assault rifle. Zulinda had some armory that I wasn't even aware of. She had been dealing with constant harassment six years before I had even started construction.

We flew the most direct flights to Frankfurt and went to ground at my apartment there. We took some side trips beer and white wine tasking. She went jovially clothes shopping and I napped. One weekend day, we drove out into the countryside and found a huge circus tent set up in a field. The parking lot was full so something interesting must be going on. We bought tickets at the tent flap and were directed to benches without backs. Our beer order was taken and then we waited. Eventually a waitress appeared with plates of steak, potatoes and the piece de resistance, asparagus. It was all you could eat, so I headed straight for the mattress when we returned. Vanna went shopping.

CHAPTER FIFTY-FOUR

Inappropriate Behavior

Two weeks later we went down on a Friday night. It was the most raucous I had ever seen Cheryl and Greg at a party. In their front room Cheryl had put out enough food for two dinners. Cases of beer cooled in the basement. Digestives lined the wall above the TV. They had other guests, one out of military and the other, Denise, salt of the earth well experienced in dealing with buzzed military fellows. Raucous in their languages, Vanna was embarrassed by the crudity when sex came up. They were ill informed. She tried to tolerate it with some Aqua Vit but we left early via Lyft to Frankfurt.

The flight to Miami was late, as typical, so we missed the connector to the island. We stayed the night in Cuenca in the better hotel on the outskirts. A delight awaited us on the island.

CHAPTER FIFTY-FIVE

Surprise Visitor

Back on the island for two days we arranged and cooperated with Roberto to get him back to farming shrimp with a vengeance. He wanted to take us over to his operation 'to see what he had' perhaps created, an unexplained twinkle.

We unbalanced my way out of the dingy and looked up near his house. A woman in a modest bikini was rocking on the porch. Roberto took Vanna's hand and walked her up the hill with me following. At first sight I thought it was Zulinda and they were going to be married. She wasn't naked. Closer, it wasn't Zulinda, 6" 5', but a match with blazing green eyes. I didn't know her at all.

"Roberto?" I was frozen expecting another jealous strapping back at the cabana if I looked astray. I think he took Vanna first so she wouldn't notice any 'discomfort' on my part. I'll admit nothing. "Roberto, who is your friend?" She moved over to him leaving no doubt as to whom she was claiming here.

Roberto started, "Lance, you know her but have never met her. Vanna, I have never talked about her during the time you have been here. I'll let her fill you in some day when you have time. Any guesses, Lance?" Hint: one only, she is Peruvian."

"Oh, you told me a saga years ago, about a pale lady from Kathmandu, but I forget the name, oh, is it Cindy?

"Yes, it is, Lance, but I am no longer the 'white lady'. Roberto's caring put that behind. On the island here, I am now the bronze lady. My English is also better due to Roberto's motivational skills. For any official purposes, I am Cynthia Maria Espinosa Martinez and now Fernandez, Cindy."

I'll quickly bring you up to date from the time Roberto and I lost and met each other. It was in Madrid after my illness from Nepal. Roberto took my care personally and nursed me back to pink/health. I was working in a software scripting company. That was my only lifeline and I had to stay when Roberto came back to his farm. Six months later he came back to see me. After one afternoon, we knew that together we must be. I resigned, took him to Peru to meet my family. We married and here we are."

"Roberto, with knowledge that you have an extra bedroom, I think we should stay tonight. I'm overwhelmed, and so proud of you Cindy, even though I've never personally met you."

Roberto had handled the introductions so deftly that Vanna had no qualms about staying. As usual, the women retired to their allotted corner of the porch. Watching their non-verbal communication did Roberto's and my hearts good.

The following day with our next joint adventure scheduled, we had a drink with Captain Brearly. He was bored again and anxious to get some U.S. mainland time with his honey. I was expecting her to be plumping up in the front anytime, but maybe they thought they were too old to deal with teenagers in 13 years. Maybe they didn't want to put her body through such difficult stresses, and the huge lumbering leading up to them.

Vanna and I were taking the dive boats out, giving the boat captains some relief. We soon worked off the good German pork. Four weeks we took ten daytime dives and a night once per week. We were exhausted from the intensity. Something could go wrong with a novice diver's B.C. trying to level off. This resort had never lost a client and that was the minimum reputation I intended to maintain. Some sleeping drug thugs did not agree. We would see some them in the distance probably causing somebody somewhere some frustration. The good captain evidently set his limits. These mini-pirates looked like products of long-time inter-marriages. Darker brown than an Afro-American with never combed scrawny braided salted hair. Sometimes an albino spot. Every chin pointed and ready to spew filthy anger.

The pressure had lessened for Roberto. Together, he and Cindy could be found out propagating shrimp. We had them for dinner or vice versa every two weeks. We learned of the famous 'Ceviche' of Peru: white-fish cooked by acidic lime juice.

Vanna gave a giggling un-stripper as she dressed. Already in competition with Cindy. I resisted and she left the cabana with Bucky to search for any items that might have come back on the bodies or firearms from the skirmish Brearly had while we were gone, items that would implicate us in any of the incidents. We had cleaned Rayban's boat the night before.

Vanna and I got into our 'night-hug" formation. We didn't wake until 10. Both dive boats were out. We went to sleep till noon. I had my own unique breakfast and we went hungrily to 'lunch'. I noticed that Bucky was not around, but figured he was on patrol after the fire fight the previous morning. Or maybe taking a well-deserved nap.

CHAPTER FIFTY-SIX

Smoke-Eaters: Fran's Boys

Fran mused, "When you are around these firemen as a group, you lump them together. You see them as one entity, not individuals. They have memorized each other's every move. A well-oiled machine! They have some things in common as most firemen must. Drenched in testosterone, if you focus on one at a time, you are struck by their abs and their rippling shoulders. That explains why they hit so many home runs on my 'Fran's Pizza Team'.

CHAPTER FIFTY-SEVEN

Fran's Phantom

I felt the soft crush on both my thighs as firm unwavering lips kissed up into a slippery of smooth damp. Then they were gone. The stalkers adoring my toned flesh softened and curled toward my thigh gap flowing on the warm film of my outer lips. The sensation of exposure did not alarm me. The sensitivity flowed further up and around my pulsing center gliding across my midriff to the base of my breasts. It coursed in circles around the buxom mounds. Roaming up the sides of each, it caused the nipples to shrink into hiding. A continued coaxing brought them back. Exploration returned its lower advance across the midriff to the pulsing heat of my sunflower. The feeling of capture by some unknown force excited me and I involuntarily began to sail to joy.

I sat up, with a start and a cry. I felt the bed. I felt no-one next to me. I was not lucid. I was in full arousal. With vibrating hand, I swiped the dampness controlling my heat, my hunger, forcing it to my right. I crashed in delight; tension dissipated. I fell back, head to pillow.

I woke up, in consternation. It was the "O". I died the glorious little death. Oh, sweet stars, but who was involved? Through my bleary eyes I looked and felt for a man in my bed. Widowed young, not a frequent but possible event. I saw a face there, but reached, finding nothing, just a memory, or a pre-cognition? There was no-one, only a face and an unusual twist of covers and pillows. I called out and got no answer. I got up to check the rooms in the apartment and found no sign of anyone nor anything. I sat again on the bed, wondering. I organized the pillows and sheets and saw some unexpected wrinkles and patterns in them. Taken close to me I decided they were the cause. Something in my mind wasn't satisfied. Another streaming flash of face. With more mundane dreams, I finished my night. The next morning, I hadn't forgotten the dream that had taken me all the way all alone. What did it portend?

I was up at 5:30 a.m. to get to my restaurant, Fran's Pizza, and deal with the inventory and tax forms. Few people were hungry for a pizza at that time of day, so I had few interruptions, except my visions flashing a dazzling phantom.

On a beer motivated unanimous decision by my men, I chartered a bus into the resorts on Key Largo and on to a Caribbean Scuba Resort. There were some inner agreements among these hotels due to the nature of tourists coming and going to the area. We occupied rooms in three different resorts. Spring break was bursting out all over and there were lots of scantily-clad co-eds cutting strays out of my pack. I couldn't help but feel jealous that my days of being the scantily clad co-ed were probably over. I was still young enough to have a baby, or two. I had some very delectable firemen and expected they would be keeping 'hands occupied', stress-free. When they were not down 30-40 feet keeping 'hands off' gorgeous coral fields flowing into the distance, that is.

I rented an 18-horse aluminum boat with two of the guys and about killed us all. I hit a reef with a propeller and broke the shear pin. We were swaying and rolling with a gentle sea, my Mexican-American fire fighter green and hanging over the railing. I saw in a first aid kit a spare shear pin. No Dramamine! I jumped into the moving currents of the reef and tried to pull the old pin out, remove the bolt to the drive shaft, bend the cotter key, inset the new pin and secure it down. I got as far as removing the bolt. Attempting to insert the new pin, a wave hit me and the new shear pin dissolved into the reef. Pins gone, no other boats in our area, out two miles into the Atlantic Ocean.

No cell phones. No way would you ever find a pin like that in the reef.

Reluctantly I moved to get up into the boat, nervous about my approaching sea-sickness. Not looking anywhere in particular other than to the center folds of the craft, I gazed and there, God or Allah or somebody had dropped another shear pin into the crevice. Easing myself back down to the reef, with spider fingers I grasped that pin and in the fear of nervousness, moved it as slow as a tug into the spherical opening. In short, saved, back on Largo, we got on our knees and kissed the earth. I never got to dive in John Penne camp Underwater State Park. But Guanaja was still ahead.

Heading back to Miami airport to fly on to San Pedro Sula and Guanaja, we were thankful for our green, now brown again Mexican-American fire fighter. With his Mexican Spanish and eye-watering girls checking out his exterior environs, we moved right through. I took the opportunity to call Vanna in the camp and review Lily's special care. Vanna sounded winded and seriously tense. We would get to the island in 4-6 hours. Maybe…. after Miami and two other airports.

Having only seen a small picture of Lily, seeing the whole package, Vanna would realize chaperoning would take precedence over training. Although Lily had practiced in a shallow lake, chaperoning did in fact soon become the norm.

CHAPTER FIFTY-EIGHT

Dreaded Attack

I was dreaming of some draught German beer and providing some lovely carved ceilings for Vanna to ponder as I pondered her. I was feeling it in the breeze and in my bones. The catastrophe of having an attack at the same time as hosting a group loomed. The destructive forces were forming. Juan Railroad had checked in with eye-witness facts. Anticipating, I had taken only one dive group for that month, Mukwonago. For the first time ever, on the second night before the Mukwonago group would arrive, I got an urgent radio call from Brealey, the captain of the Artificial Island, Floating Suburbia.

CHAPTER FIFTY-NINE

Company-Sized Cartel Attack

Brearly, "Birdcage, we've got bogies coming in from the mainland and others from Drug Island. There appear to be four diesels and a half a dozen under-water transporter. ETA, one to one and half hours. Biggest attack ever. The transporters are heading toward Zulinda's beach, also two diesels. I may bring in two helicopters. Over!"

"Black Bird, contact Cuenca airport and shut down all Guanaja flights until further notice. I know your clientele moguls will have influence there.

Roberto, Vanna and I had agreed that if such a raid took place, and if we survived, we needed to take the fighting to them. Roberto had bought the shrimp fields and in closing received maps of all the lot lines on the island including the large fort. I flew the drone over the fort at altitude, and located what appeared to be the room large enough to hold armaments and ammunition.

Vanna said, "We are dealing with a large group of greedy bastards, and we can't go in there and expect with our small numbers to neutralize them all. From the pictures, I can quickly devise explosive charges that should combine with what they have in there and bring that part of the fort down. The drone is powerful enough to take what we need in two trips. If the time comes and we see them moving our way to attack, we must send the first drone load as they are leaving the shore. Lance, I assume you can deliver the load right on target. The second load must go immediately so you can get the drone back to support the battle.

The time was the worst possible. Songbird sensed it. Bucky began growling as he patrolled the beaches. Roberto was behaving at Zulinda's now he was married.

I called him back and told her to prepare whatever she had. Octavio was heading home in the early morning after collecting "$2000" for the day. He reversed at full plane. Distances involved put him in Zulinda's cove with minutes to spare. I went down and recruited the boat captains. They got suppressed-fire rifles from the boats. They had been wearing pistols on their belts for a week.

I went through the thickets and thorns to the top of the hill between the resorts. I sent the drone to surveil. Surprisingly Songbird had called the beginning. I had stopped communicating with Brainerd long ago. They came back concerned that there were seven boats coming mostly manned by three crooks apiece. My drone called five boats headed for the dive resort and two toward Zulinda. Vanna was on the ridge of the hill to the west. Roberto was at the veranda at the top of the resort. I informed Vanna and asked her to forward the information to Zulinda. I had long ago got out from between them, even in battle.

Lance feels Songbird out, "Songbird, they are definitely on their way. Can you begin support? Over."

"Birdcage, we can't respond until we confirm they are actually feet down on the island. Over."

With a building rage inside, I wanted to drench with curses the congress who controlled these drones with such worldly unawareness and stupidity. I held my tongue and didn't respond to anyone.

Vanna replied with more patience than I could muster, "This is birdcage, all the help as soon as you can would be welcome. We'll defend and clean-up. Standing bye."

"Lance, I'll call Zulinda."

Lance adds, "Octavio, are you out fishing, yet?"

Quick response. "I'm out and I also saw your Mukwonago tour group in Cuenca airport. Brearly closed it. Be there in a half hour. Automatic weapons, rifles and two small depth charges prepared."

"Roberto, bogies coming from shore and Drug Island. Approximately ten craft, maybe twelve. Bring the RPG's. Artificial Island is responding with two helicopters. Hurry over, buddy!"

Now an hour of waiting. Octavio arrived first and took station on the east end of Zulinda's beach. The beach was composed of several bamboo roofs, a toilet, and two changing rooms with no walls. If it's a nude beach, why have walls on a changing room? There was one concrete building with roof where the kitchen was located.

Vanna had reached Zulinda who was crawling out in her sans-dress, dragging the latest guy also disrobed onto the sand. The two got the other staff who herded the clients up in the trees toward Starr Resort.

I was back on the drone, honing in on the underwater transporters coming from the Drug Island. The green laser was charging directly off the big generator.

Zulinda, a true vision, body whirling down to where she had a bunker with weapons such as I have never seen off a military base. Her staff arrived and she handed out weapons and sent them to the most effective firing positions. Some went to the trees; three to sand hills in front of the kitchen.

"Vanna, sitrep?"

"Birdcage, one submersible tried to slip by. Trey hit it with an RPG, I am 'shooting gallery' the others. One other diesel has a remaining thug ducking and screaming. A suicide runs to our beach. Oops, SWAT flattened him.

"Vanna, you've got to defend the west of our beach. SWAT has to move east. Give the boat captain the other RPGs. Do you have a suppressed riffle you can give Trey? Follow in case any thug resurfaces. Put Trey back on your shooting gallery. We could really use Bucky here."

"Black Bird, do you see the suicide boat heading toward our dock? Support please."

"Black bird, now you see them, green ray, now you don't. Some clean-up will be needed before your clients hit the beach in the morning. I've decimated any floating object near Zulinda."

"Thank you, Black Bird, much obliged"

"Zulinda, Sitrep."

"Lance, all but one down. One got away into the woods, coming your way. I've sent Tim after him but it's hard to run through the barbs naked. Expect him. Big scar on his cheek, unruly blond hair. He's gonna be too close to use the drone."

"Got it! The thug also has thorn trouble. He'll never suffer from that again. Over."

"Vanna, could you get Trey and Boat Captains to help you get the bodies into the tug boats. If you need more room, use our security boat. Tow them around the corner well north of our dock while we clean up here. We have so many, and a Mondo. We'll protect Octavio's cruiser with a canvass tarp to make the Davy Jones Trip."

"Lance, Black bird here, it's done with one injury on our staff. One boat captain has a flesh would but the bullet missed the bone. Vanna or Zulinda can handle it. We're here to clean up the beach.

Lance, "Black Bird, "Our Valhalla load is going soon. Do you have any donations? Over"

"Birdcage, one of our guys got it in the arm. He's patched up and will be fine. If it turns out I have extra refuse, my chopper will follow your boat to the deep. Get some sleep now. Out."

"Black Bird, please reopen the airport for Mukwonago Tell them not to authorize flights to Guanaja until after three p.m."

"Roger that, Birdcage. Out."

After dark with the lamps glowing distantly, Rayban and Roberto scouted the beaches and nearby wooded areas for any munitions or objects left from the fight.

Vanna and I got into our 'night-hug" formation and didn't wake until 10. Both dive boats were out. We went to sleep till noon. I had my own unique wake-up and then we went to 'lunch'. I noticed that Bucky was not around, but figured he was on patrol after the fire fight the previous night. Or maybe taking a well-deserved nap.

CHAPTER SIXTY

Delay in Cuenca

Delay in Miami, one hour. Nothing new. Fran expected an hour, maybe two. At two in the morning, without explanation, they put us on two planes and re-routed us to Cuenca. A bus there took us to a hotel on the main road into town. There they left us, so we went to bed.

Breakfast consisted of refried beans on deep-fat fried plantain and Nescafe with or without milk. The meal went slowly as did the bus on the way back to the airport. Following the palms and pineapples on each side of the road, slow as we were going, I saw very clearly, we passed the entrance to the airport. No one except me reacted. The driver said nothing, even to our Spanish Speaking fire fighter. I surged up out of my seatbelt to get to him and get some explanation. All the driver repeated was, "somebody coming". "Good time."

My group was beginning to react and I had no doubt we would soon have a burly fire truck driver doing a U-Turn back to the airport. The driver turned left quickly out onto a service road and stopped among acres of pineapples.

Bus stopped, a short but fluent, intelligent native of the north coast, hopped up and said quickly, "My name is Juan Olivera. Due to some services, I provide for your island host, Lance, sometimes associated with the railroads, he calls me Juan Railroad. Today, I have a more delightful pleasure of taking you on a short side trip before we head to the island. It is unusual and the full explanation you deserve is that a celluloid on one of the air compressors has worn out. The part is available on the mainland and will be installed in time for dinner tonight. In the meantime, we have some pineapples to taste, a romantic water falls to cool us off and wine with lunch. I know this may come as a shock, so I am giving your leader a copy of my Honduran I.D and my U.S. visa to establish your security. I assure you this will be a delightful day, so hop off the bus and let's get into some juicy pineapple tasting."

With promised style and cooking skills, Juan provided a memorable day. The romance of the waterfall was muted by my being the only woman and a couple of the guys already married.

As the sun went down, the winds luffed and mosquitos took over the area. We hurried back to make the flight before the wind changed again.

CHAPTER SIXTY-ONE

Fran Collapse-Phantom at Starr Resort

The resort was on a different island than the runway. The boat that picked us up was shades of the ghosts of Key Largo. It was diesel and the boat captain who picked us up, familiar, probably knew every meter of reef within miles. We arrived at the three-prong dive boat pier, 'ungreened', and unloaded.

Lance and Vanna along with two dive boat captains and another handsome driver staff member welcomed us. I was balancing Lily and organizing her suitcases so didn't pay attention until Lance spoke. He had a deep voice that demanded attention.

"Welcome, Fran, we thank you for your service, firemen", Lance greeted. Juggling hers and Lily's equipment, Fran glanced up to smile at Lance, looked over his shoulder, lurched, and fell to her knees. Huge eyes. Ragged breaths! A dozen fully trained EMT's surrounded her. Lily, spread legs with swimmers' thighs, raised her back to her feet. They checked whatever could be checked with her clothes on and Roberto's Cindy stayed with her in the bungalow shared with Lily.

Vanna saw the other woman Lance hadn't had a chance to welcome and surprised at her developed feminine body said, "Welcome Lily, I'm Vanna." Smiles met smiles but Lily was dizzy in the jungle-meets-beach surroundings."

The firemen and captains carried the equipment to the ramp boats and the cabanas. Lance put everyone to a nap and promised to wake them for happy hour and dinner. There would be no tank diving today but they could snorkel out toward the east end of the island if they couldn't sleep.

Concerned, but Trey made a point of being the one to settle Fran and Lily. He brought the slough of suitcases they had up to the bungalow. Cindy was still with Fran as she focused into the muffled light. Trey smiled at Fran who jerked and tensed again, fell back, and closed her eyes.

Fran reacted to all the mauling and whispering going on around her. "Look, we don't know each other well enough for all this. I have talked twice to Vanna on the phone and only have met Cindy now. I know what I told you about your Trey, and I am not insane. I own and manage a successful restaurant with one other waitress, Lily and a cook. Lily's sister comes in to help if we expect a crowd. I am charming and endearing with the customers. I do all business operations, auditing, ordering, and inventory. I've been married but am now a widow. It was a heartbreaking loss. I date occasionally. That's enough for you to know to take me diving. Sorry, I guess the jet lag made me a little irritable.

Vanna brought Lily up to their bungalow where Fran had cleared her eyes from her second siting of Trey. Cindy stayed a few minutes to settle the two into camp life.

The next day Vanna met with Fran to learn the idiosyncrasies of Lily. Lily, who had developed into a mouthwatering beauty had, in her early teen years, some malady in brain development. During early years and for some time into the teens, there is a series of growth spurts that enhance brain function. For Lily, the spurt that normally happens at about 13 years didn't, or didn't complete itself. Her geometry teacher was first to notice it. If functioning, it would enhance Lily's ability to imagine and, in her mind, see three dimensional shapes. She could imagine those shapes opening to their component parts. Perhaps related, she had some trouble manipulating the four most basic operations on numbers: adding, subtracting, multiplying, and dividing. She had no interest in a career in mathematics so the teacher gave her "CA", credit awarded on her course list which gave her a high school diploma. With the advent of calculators, Lily, after repeated drills, could get answers needed most of the time.

Her mother passed away and she fell to the loving hands of her older sister. The sister was running Fran's Pizza restaurant so Fran could get a vacation after her painful loss of a young husband and get Lily out to see there was more than Mukwonago in the world. The sister had been with Fran since graduation, developing a plan for a pizza restaurant in teenaged plagued downtown Mukwonago. The sister would be an investor and Fran would be CFO. In the deal. Lily would have a job waitressing. Along with the calculator came the cash register computer, opening further success for her in her job. Even the computer didn't solve all of the difficulties, but with a 15-minute refresher each Monday morning, Lily operated usually successfully. There wasn't a male customer who wouldn't forgive and help such an Aphrodite with a billing error. Along with the salary she would earn tips, more needn't be said, for a living that could support her with some pride, but a captivating innocence.

The growth spurt didn't miss the rest of her development, so the sister and Fran had to watch the advent of boys. Lily was a swimming pool fish since her earliest years. By her graduation, the swimming had toned her legs making her more of a danger to the male population, and her sister. She had called on that strength when Fran swooned on the pier. She side-stepped and pulled her right up. With a good friend in her boss, Fran, she was excited about joining scuba training in the pool and in shallow lakes in the region.

With Vanna up-dated, she got Lily and took her for a warm-up shallow water snorkel. Cindy urged Fran to get a suit on and dive into the surf but kept Lily nearby when Vanna excused herself.

Vanna found Trey up cleaning the leaves and branches around Fran's bungalow.

"Trey, do you know this Fran from someplace?"

"I don't recall ever seeing her before. She is a real fox and I doubt I would have forgotten that."

"Have you ever been to Mukwonago, your last three-week vacation, for example, or in an airport there, or a connector to Chicago?"

"Vanna, I am sincere about this. I have never even been to Wisconsin. It's a cold state most of the year with few lakes with visibility for diving. There is a deep lake, Lake Michigan on the east of the state, but again little visibility. Its so cold people say you can't even get comfortable in a full suit."

"Curious!"

"Vanna, I have never even seen this "Mukwonago" name before and doubt I could pronounce it correctly.

"Ok, Trey, sorry to grill you, Fran thinks she saw you in a dream as a phantom or some such."

"Vanna, at a good time I will go and introduce myself and see if she wants to put her hand through my chest. No, seriously, I will try to help her feel safe. Not crying or fainting, she's a fox, still."

CHAPTER SIXTY-TWO

Phantom Unearthed

In the ensuing twilight, Trey and Fran were over at the wall practicing gymnastics. He had approached her and, keeping his distance, introduced himself, saying they wouldn't need a pick-up line because they had the 'phantom' in common. Fran was not inclined to question after a few more glances at him, and checking he really was flesh and blood, and six-packs. Not interested in living alone forever, she chose the tiger-striped thong for a moon-light dip. She had no transparent wrap to wear before or after dipping. Trey was all eyes. Lily slept alone until late.

In this scuba-designed situation, there was potential danger so all kept an eye on lily. Fran had gotten scuba lessons for her in a pool in Mukwonago. She was excited to do it. Vanna took her by the hand and helped her warm up by snorkeling around the reef down the beach. She put the tank on and went to four meters watching her clear her ears and managing the B.C. Vanna had to swoop in to punch a demanding thump to her chest to get her to exhale when ascending.

"Lily sputtered, yes, yes, I know that. I don't want to explode."

"Then do it!"

They did it again. Then five more times. Vanna was doggedly protecting our reputation; and Lily's life.

The following day, Lily, running on 7 of her 8 cylinders, swam laps around the dock while Vanna loaded her equipment. The dive would be to the wall where good sea life and colored novice-reef were at 10-30 feet. Vanna would keep her away from the wall.

Trey and Fran were already over at the wall practicing now suggestive gymnastics.

Lily hadn't practiced entering the water from the boat but the ramps made that easy. Vanna sat beside her, balancing her, getting her regulator set; putting her hand on the BC. She was talking, encouraging her; reminding her; trying to make her relax. They both eased into the water. Vanna set her B.C. and went to check Lily's. Lily hadn't adjusted it so Vanna did. They floated along beside the boat; Vanna took her elbow and eased her down to 10 feet.

We hadn't known in advance the amount of monitoring Lily would need. Vanna had to be in hot blood to catch every unthinking mistake Lily could make. Watching Vanna fly, I considered changing some resort policies.

No decompression would be needed for this depth. They looked around at the bottom of the boat, saw Fran and Trey in the distance. From under the transom in a wash of bubbles a barracuda shot out swerving toward them and as a flash into the distance. Lily squeezed her BC, screamed bubbles out under her mask and shot up shouting and spluttering. At least the screams prevented an embolism.

Lily was in tears saying, "that's enough, take me out, there are monsters. The pool in Mukwonago doesn't have monsters. Help, help", flailing around with her tank pulling her down. Vanna leaped and had her weight belt and tank off in a flash. She put her in a lifesaving hold and got her around and up on the ramp. Fran and Trey were oblivious, but that was no fault of theirs. It was our call so Vanna got the rest of her equipment off and comforted her until the divers returned after 45 minutes.

Worried, Fran came up the ramp responding to Lily's tears. Vanna explained, Lily said she only wanted to snorkel by the little reef she had been at the day before. The next morning, Vanna coated her with sun protection and spent two rounds of snorkeling, morning and afternoon. Lily spent the rest of the week swimming around the rafts and riding the boats while others dived.

Fran and Trey continued to be diving buddies. Interesting what can be done in buoyant salt water.

The next day, Vanna and I went to happy hour. We weren't diving the next day. Cook made a super grasshopper with ice cream so we each had one on the veranda. Trey and Fran came up and talked with us for a while. I could see his discomfort, knew it well for what it was. We soon left to our cabin; in case it might be contagious. This time, as I looked over my shoulder, they were in a deep kiss on the path on the way to his cabin.

At breakfast the next morning, there were two sets of, what do they call them in Wisconsin, 'Cow eyes. I have to confess, Vanna and I sported one set.

Camp Owner Lance, I went down to open their first dives warning the firemen about too much beer and too many atmospheres. They all had used a variety of air and oxygen tanks, but few underwater. Fran had gone down deep in Lake Superior.

The camp regimen promised in our brochure was two dives per day, morning and afternoon and a night dive once per week, pending wind conditions. For the average sport diver, this is a bit stressful. These fire guys are not average anything and hit every dive. Lily was off in her 'never, never' world supervised by Vanna.

When Fran succumbed after six dives, Trey of course was 'tired', too. She went up and got her bikini. They snorkeled and tanned on the famous east end of the island. The bikini absolutely screamed description. The ink in this paragraph would cover more than the suit.

There is some thought that mid-west girls tend to be conservative. Fran was far from being a teenager; she had lost a man she really adored. She had no intention of living alone all her life. The bikini was a thong with a bra that only hinted at holding anything in check. Tiger spot designs hammered the point home.

I still had to be careful about what Vanna might notice me viewing. That may be a life sentence. A dirty look and I headed upstairs for a snack. The morning dive came in and lunch was served. The guys flopped down to power nap, but Fran and Trey didn't arrive. We could see their splashes in the distance with occasional no-splash sun bathing. No worries.

CHAPTER SIXTY-THREE

Dive and Fight

A day to decompress Lily's mind, the second dive, Lily and Vanna aboard, headed out to the North of the island where some bigger fish hung about. I stayed on the dock with a cold beer and thick sun screen applied by Vanna. After twenty minutes on each side, I moved onto the boardwalk up to the bar under the shade of some primeval trees. I had been out for two hours. First Fran and then Trey in the distance headed back, some more clothed than others. The eastern edge of Zulinda's resort, Unclad.com, that is, may have been influential.

A refreshing night in camp, Fran and I were sitting at the happy hour bar deeply engaged in sharing diving adventures around the mid-west. Trey was on the other side of Fran, and Fran was dressed for him. Dressed for him, but right next to me. She was not a Vanna, nor even a Zulinda, but she was a stocky mid-western girl well endowed. Smart, she owned her own business. Probably a Norwegian in the gene pool; warm, loving blue eyes. The stocky didn't interfere with the right curves in the right places. I wasn't enveloped in side looks at her breasts. I was focused on the diving in the Racine quarry, a dirty dive with rusted cars; no visibility. My chair was rammed in no uncertain terms away from Fran, and Vanna plunked herself in hot blood between us. With an embarrassed pause, I finished the discussion of the quarry and turned away. Fran turned back to Trey.

In honor of guys from beef states, the cook bar-b-queued racks of Angus ribs. Fresh mixed salads and baked potatoes rounded it off. Light on drinks. Vanna selected a table well away from them. Nothing was said. I would rather have her over-protective than disinterested. Vanna should remember my touch and adoration for her by now and not be so quick to attack either the object of my glance or conversation. Dangerous as a Navy Seal, maybe she was also Irish. I had proved over and over she was THE object of my affection.

We got drinks and went up to the veranda watching the moon. Trey and Fran arrived, well plastered against each other. We respected their privacy and headed up to our cabin. I looked over my shoulder and this time he had her bra in his teeth, ushering her into his bungalow. Having seen the tiger spot bikini in action, I quickly turned away. Fast enough for the eyes on me and turns out, I had been forgiven. I had behaved in a pristine manner after the dive-sharing with Fran. The A/C covered intensely delivered sparks and moans.

CHAPTER SIXTY-FOUR

Bucky Hurt

Our comfortable bubble was interrupted. Bucky came to sleep with us occasionally. It happened after one of our skirmishes. I guess he figured there wouldn't be anything more, otherwise he would be on guard. That wasn't the case tonight. He came in with a hard limp, a heart rendering whine, and blood in the hair of his back left leg.

Vanna reacted quickly and lovingly devised a sling for the leg. She gave him some people pain relievers and I called Roberto. Woke him up. He would come over early tomorrow and take him to Alicia Maria, the vet on the coast between Ceiba and United fruit. We put him in the bed with us to keep him comfortable from the A/C. Vanna gave him another pain pill at 5:00 a.m.

It may not be typical for a big Alpha male like me to feel so close to a dog. I was there when he was born at Alicia's kennel. As soon as he was ready, we had Alicia train him to be the alarm clock of the camp if trouble was scented. He also was tutored to be a protective force if he sensed danger.

CHAPTER SIXTY-FIVE

Bucky's Secret:

Bucky healed and saved many islanders from unsuspecting Thugs. No one knows for sure how he got the injury when the ensuing Mukwonago was in camp. Up on the hill beyond the camp, he lunged at a Don J mafia Vanna had missed, saving Vanna. Vanna dispatched the thug but didn't see Bucky's injury. It took him two nights pulling his broken leg behind him to get to Vanna's cabana. Vanna used first aid and sent him to Alicia for re-training never realizing Bucky had saved her so she could dispatch her threatening feral father in law, Don J.

CHAPTER SIXTY-SIX

Saving of Lily and Wooing of Fran

Vanna and Bucky finished their circuit and checked for any lagging snorkelers. Vanna and the boat captain, who had guarded the camp yesterday, would lead the morning dives. I would sub in for Vanna in the afternoon who would work with Lily.

The firemen were used to Lily in a variety of sexy attire and ignored her. They had about as much interest as the Germans in Melissa. There were only a couple other men working. Both on the morning and afternoon dives, Trey and Fran were quickly buddies.

After dinner, Vanna and I went up on the veranda. Soon another couple appeared. Fran and Trey focused seriously on each other's eyes wandered up the back steps. We quietly and quickly said good night and headed for our cabin. Heading up to the cabin with Vanna, I turned back and saw them saying good-night with one kiss, but one of merit. They went separately to their cabins. Lily was already down.

Nothing was said. I guess I would rather have her over-protective of me than disinterested. Vanna should remember my touch and adoration for her. I told her about the battle starting out to the west.

"We should go, Lance."

"Honey, I've got Roberto, Rayban, his armory and maybe Zulinda. Brearly is also aware. If they get within 50 feet of his island, he has authorization to take them out. If they need help, we can be there in ten minutes in the Chevy. I got the radio, let's go up on the veranda and try to keep folks down here or on the beach. You can be kissing me and embarrass them back down. We can go up to the tower if we start hearing explosions. Maybe give some intel. If they move closer, we'll meet them with the Chevy."

We got drinks and went up to the veranda watching the moon. Trey and Fran appeared; they were a single person with four legs. Lily would be sleeping alone in Fran's bungalow tonight.

As they went in, I heard the first roar of several muted explosions. The RPG's. If that hadn't been enough, we didn't have many heavy munitions left. I had forgotten clearly. I realized that and relaxed. I listened for the suppressors but they were doing their job, we couldn't hear them. A few minutes, seconds really, later, the Mexican-American guy came rumbling up. He stopped next to us back on the tower. He listened for several seconds.

"Lance, you can tell these people whatever you want if they hear the explosions over there. But I know damn well that no army training drills are ever anywhere near here. I was born in Central America. There's an extended runway in Cuenca. America built it. Nobody is going to be doing a 'fucking" thing on it if a dozen trucks and helicopters with U.S. flags waving aren't there. I'll keep my mouth shut if you confirm none of these people here are going to be hurt."

"Jorge, we have protecting forces against some drug marauders in that area. The last two explosions were the end of that battle. I'll be getting a sitrep in ten to twenty minutes. All are safe here. Good evening."

Octavio came on in five minutes. "No survivors, no escapees. We're heading out to 400 feet and will meet with you tomorrow."

"Our group will leave at noon before the winds come up. Come any time after two. But Roberto, take several of the heavy weaponry from Rayban and store them. He can get more, cheap, from Frumpland, liar of the home-grown White Supremacists."

"Roger, out."

CHAPTER SIXTY-SEVEN

Sneak Attack; Mukwonago at Camp

Next morning, moving quietly up toward our cabana, I got a radio call from Roberto. "We got a group of three smoke pots with three pirates in each. Maybe remnants of last night. I know you have a big group from the mid-west now. How do you want to handle it? We have an hour and a half."

"I could probably get away, but Vanna will scalp me if I leave her alone with this group. She's got a bombshell young woman, short a brick for a full roof, who keeps her hopping. It would be good if you can do this without me, unless an unexpected emergency requires. Do you have some armament?"

"Not much, and not enough. I only have two RPG's and two sound-suppressed rifles and one revolver. And Bucky, of course, but I'm afraid we could seriously endanger him."

"Call Octavio and see where he is. He's fully loaded. Call me back immediately with the info. I hope he's not in Sambo Creek."

"Birdcage, some luck finally today. He's leaving Zulinda. Will be back in 20 minutes. He might be able to bring Zulinda.

"Ok on Zulinda, but no pressure on her. This isn't her fight. Octavio is going to have some heavy equipment, loud equipment. Try to start the attack as far west keeping noise east of airport island. Are you ok with this, Roberto?

"After what I went through last night and I'm still here, I figure I'm ok."

"Try to box the invasion to the west. I think you should leave for the east of Roadan in 20 minutes. Good luck, be careful and call me back with a sitrep as soon as you have them neutralized. Out."

One fight we didn't personally have to face. And no injured had been mentioned. The A/C covered some intensely delivered sparks and moans. Mostly Vanna, of course.

CHAPTER SIXTY-EIGHT

Alicia and Cesarito

In the failed state where we lived, I was very cautious choosing a doctor, or a retailer, or a vet with all the cartel lackeys around. I almost didn't choose Alicia. I used a contact in the embassy to do a background check on her. She was pristine clean, but she was married to the son of one of the most infamous drug lords in the area. I contacted Juan of the Railroad Street Regulars. His knowledge of her background saved her a new client. Bucky was born two weeks after she returned from Texas A & M. That summer she taught him to be a protection dog with two weeks in being an attack dog.

Alicia Maria, was from a wealthy family well founded for generations, long before the cartel. She was academically a shining star in all her elementary and secondary English-medium education. She had 4.0 grade point average and scores at the top of the SAT I and II's. She was all over the community charity work, partly because her family was so wealthy. The family was well-prepared to handle her university costs, but she was given a full ride at Texas A&M.

She even met with the admissions committee to describe her family's situation, and no need of extra help. The response was firmly:

"This is not based on need, this is based on the excellence you have shown as an academic and a caring community member. We have no doubt about your potential of success and frankly, we think you may be a resource and interesting support to your classmates. We are not going to lose you to the University of Houston, nor Oklahoma State without a struggle."

The die was cast and she became all she is and what they hoped for.

The Don J. Mondo had a boy at her class level. Ceasrito, a handsome youngster but naïve and only moderate in ability. He had some unusual abilities to memorize. He couldn't analyze what he knew. That wasn't enough to gain a scholarship. The Mondo extorted the teachers to give false, successful grades. Threats to family members. The Don J. Mondo also went to the gift coordinator at Oklahoma Ag. and built an addition of private practice and study rooms to the library. Ceasrito was welcomed with opened arms. He never saw or didn't realize that part of the library had his name on it.

Many undergrad classes could be passed with memorization skills; he got by. He went to a summer combined seminar for potential veterinarians including universities in western U.S. Texas A&M was there. Alicia was there. She was brilliant and beautiful and he was built and pretty. Before the end of the first date, she recognized the academic and analysis skill he didn't have. But plenty of girls choose fewer academic mates.

They lived on the north coast only forty miles apart so in summers they would be seeing each other again. After the seminar, he returned to Sula looking for summer work. There was a vet with property and horses a few miles east of the Copan Ruins. He had advertised for summer help. Ceasrito mentioned the job in the family and before he could go to interview, one of the lieutenants had visited. There would be no interview. Ceasrito would be given the job.

"Oh, look at your lovely wife and daughters. It would be terrible if any accident should happen to them."

Pure, blatant extortion! Fine-tuned in the not so hallowed halls of northern neighbor's congress.

The vet had been there for years. He knew it was a land

of no legal recourse. Unaware, Ceasrito reported for work. He didn't understand why he got such a cold welcome, but started, following directions and being cooperative. He loved working with horses and was kind and supportive. The vet had some hope for this boy in the short run.

The next summer, Ceasrito contacted the vet to work again. The lieutenant visited again with his not so veiled threats and Ceasrito started again. The vet quietly moved to downsize the business, or sell it, the following year. Either way there would be no need for a cartel boy to be employed. The family would probably have to move away as well. They did, to the Guatemalan border.

The senior year was a year of a platonic relationship between Alicia Marie and Ceasrito in spite of the intellectual difference. Alicia had worked again with parent support to finalize the veterinary hospital. She could graduate right into her office with the license on the wall. In fact, she did.

In March of her senior year, she learned that Ceasrito was Cartel. The relationship stalled, cooled. He was heartbroken with no realization of what the problem was.

Alicia knew of the criminal extortions of the cartel and would not be so stupid as to tell the crime boss's son why she was balking. He was so unworldly aware he might unintentionally cry to his father and get her killed or at least her business destroyed.

She stayed awake nights pondering and analyzing what could be salvaged, if anything:

1. He was kind to people and animals all.

2. He had fallen completely under her influence.

3. They could practice veterinary together with her interest in small pets and dogs and his in horses.

4. He was not schooled in the higher arts or dance. On the other hand, he was an excellent dancer. Enthralling even.

5. She had never considered buying a new pair of shoes before trying them on, so any future bed-play had to test explosive. There was time.

6. His unique memory skills would cover her friend's doubt in her choice of him.

7. To wake up each morning to the adoration in his eyes was stunning.

Refocusing on the darker aspects she would face; she was sure his father would do no harm to his son's wife. He would also not damage a veterinary office that offered his son a career that he had the mental ability to handle. She faced the discomfort she would meet in attending family parties and business discussions. In a life-threatening emergency, her own family could try to protect her.

Carrying a torch for her, Ceasrito could be influenced to give her all she wanted. She also steeled herself for the worst because any divorce would be a death penalty. With his adoration, few problems between them occurred. She wore the pants in this couple and got what she wanted.

She slowly began to accept his invitations to date again, but sleeping together was put on hold perhaps until after they were married. The increase in his hunger caused him to relent to her every whim. Every unfilled night more.

She soon learned of the boredom and disgusting activities of the cartel ladies' club and their laudatory remarks about how clever their husbands were in business extortion. They considered non-cartel families, a lower class to be taxed and taken advantage of for Cartel comforts. Shades of modern-day re-inequality for blacks or browns.

She immediately stopped going to the lady's club despite many efforts to get her back. She went once when anyone missing would be expelled. Ceasrito did whatever she wanted in all things and everything. She left meetings as soon as she would not be missed.

CHAPTER SIXTY-NINE

No Way in Hell Will Alicia Be Trounced

The Donny J. Mondo hated her. He knew her roots and soon realized her striking intelligence. Both were a danger to him. She was a F==king woman; "Batt and I traffic that shit!"

He and the present trophy step-mother staged a war against her. Shameful slurs came at her from all sides:

"Quechua bitch, Inca sucker, animal pedophile, Mayan Whore," lessons from the North. Lackeys and wives were kissing his Don J. feet for their fear of what he and his allies could do to them. Extortion, lies and dirty money spread on the community.

Incensed, Alicia fired the love-making to hot and hard and right now and thrilling. No wait for marriage. There was no way she would be defeated in this conspiracy. Ceasrito was ever under her spell; needed her arms. He went. She responded lovingly. She gave him his deep desire and in the loving bubble afterwards, they (she) scheduled the wedding for two weeks later. She charmed him and he fought his father's distaste. She influenced and he forced the mother to plan the ceremony.

Alicia held him in deep kisses and demanded that the wedding only include immediate family. The relationship was going as she had analyzed. Her joy in his adoration grew and became the most elusive tool.

They had been married three years. She heard another bigger raid would be carried out against the Guanaja groups. She mentioned it to Ceasrito. He said, "Yeah, my dad's going on this one. He thinks they need more motivation to win this time. They are taking some underwater diver transports."

Alicia informed Roberto that evening.

CHAPTER SEVENTY

Mondo Down, Limbo for Alicia

The cartel invasion began the following day. Cesearito had nothing to do with the cartel. He was sickened at what his father was fomenting. The distance couldn't have been further between father and son. Ceasrito was making a pair of horse shoes that afternoon.

Rayban roared into the inlet of the veterinary kennel with Bucky. The Don J. Mondo, Ceasritos' father, in his flaunted dress had been the last one off the boat near the airport. Bucky took him down so Vanna could get a safe shot. Don J. took a diver's knife swinging at Bucky's rear right leg. In a second, a double tap ended the fight and the existence of such evil. Vanna was under fire from behind so she turned and flattened, not noticing Bucky's injury. No correlation between the two incidents was ever uncovered.

I knew. I knew that Bucky had laid in the woods two days trying to lick his wound. A healing dog's tongue is not enough for a broken bone. Bucky finally came, whining and dragging his back leg to us in bed in our cabin. Roberto, who knew Alicia, the vet, from elementary school days, responded. The medical recovery required extended time and therapy. He had to be taken to his original guard dog level of response back to the attack dog level. Three months later, he was barking and excited to be back on the island with his human friends.

Three days later, no one returned from the raid. No Don J. Mondo. No correlation between Bucky's attack and Alicia's medical care for the dog that took out her hated father-in-law.

CHAPTER SEVENTY-ONE

Lives Reset

Alicia had to reset and consider what her situation might be with a strange new Don J. Mondo. She again spoke with her father. His years of experience in this sickened society provided an answer, at least short term.

"No Mondo would harm a previous Mondo's son. The ugly relations among family cartel members at least didn't permit that."

It was an advantage that Mondo's were disappearing so often in the islands. Scheming, she would shimmer out "wet lightning" to drive Ceasrito slowly out of his mind whenever it suited her. She would make greater damage to the Cartel, sometime, someday.

CHAPTER SEVENTY-TWO

Love Confirmed

Bucky was gone with Roberto and his wife, Cindy. Early in the morning a sheepish looking Trey walked to our table and sat down.

"Lance, Vanna, it would be sorely anticlimactic for me to review the fun and fright I have shared with you. I will wait for the promised two weeks, but then I have some Pizza to deliver in Mukwonago, and a sweet young girl to protect from guys like me. Maybe some fire-department training: using a tank above the water. I can pronounce the name now. It's in the lips."

We all smiled and congratulated him. Every one of us knew, Fran would never let him out of her arms, or away from her lips.

Lance glances, "I could see in Trey's stance how disappointed he was, not going with them that next noon. He would have to weather another attack. Both Railroad Juan and Sarah's intel concurred. I saw the invasion size; I put him up in the Drone tower. Effective shooter and located safely, I wanted to assure he would make that dream for Fran and Lily come true."

CHAPTER SEVENTY-THREE

Last Bow for Trey, Much to Live For

"Birdcage, this is Black Bird, we've got bogies coming in from the mainland and others from Drug Island. Five diesels and a half a dozen under-water transporter. ETA, one hour. Their transporters are heading toward both resorts. I may bring in two helicopters. Over!"

Vanna replied, "This is birdcage, the help would be welcome. Standing bye."

"Lance, try to get Octavio and Roberto. I'll wake the captains and see if I can find Trey. I'll call Zulinda."

"Octavio, are you out fishing, yet?"

"Birdcage, I'm out and will be there in a half hour. Automatic weapons, rifles and two small depth charges prepared."

"Roberto, wake up. Bogies coming from shore and Drug Island. Approximately ten craft, maybe twelve. Intel says we got a Mondo. Bring the RPG's. Artificial Island is responding with two helicopters, but they need some time. We have to hold until they can get here."

Now an hour of waiting. Octavio arrived first and took station on the east end of Zulinda's beach. Vanna rousted Zulinda crawling out in her not-a-stitch body. The two got the other staff and guests herded into safety. This was the worst-case scenario when guests, who might talk to others, would not have positive things to say. Starr was lucky; we had just sent

Mukwonago home.

Trey was on the drone targeting green ray, honing in on the underwater transporters coming from Drug Island. Zulinda ran down to the west end of her beach, bouncing a glorious vision, where she had a bunker with weapons such as I have never seen outside of a military weapons cache.

"Black bird, we are in place. In ten minutes, Trey will start taking out the underwater transporters nearest you. They show up clearly on his drone screen. Over."

"Negative, Bird Cage, hold fifteen and let me take the helicopters in to deliver impulsion mines. When I finish, Trey can take out what's left while I land the helicopters. Safer all around. It looks like you and Zulinda are going to get three diesels with three thugs each. I'll disembark two SWAT guys near the airport away from your dock. Three to Zulinda. Over."

Lance responds, "Roger, thank the Force, Mukwonago is gone."

Lance re-engages, "Vanna, meet the SWAT guys at the west end near the island channel. That's where the thugs always try to sneak in. Bucky can lead that charge. Leave Trey in the tower. I'm not gonna send him home damaged goods. Take three RPG's. Shoot as soon as their boats come into site. You can call in a strike from Trey, or have SWAT launch, but we've got to neutralize those to protect our resort. Send SWAT to back-up Zulinda. She has guests and we don't so she may take an undeserved marketing hit."

Lance orders, "Boat captains, watch for submersibles. Both SWAT and we have drone finders to locate them. Call me if you see one that is not already burning. I'll have Trey clear it. We've got to keep the pier and the resort free from any sign of conflict."

Bodie, boat captain growls, "They'll enter here over our dead bodies. Concentrate on your major assault and rest assured we will handle with dispatch anything that comes our way."

"Bodie, above and beyond your call of duty, but sincere thanks", Lance tense voice.

"Octavio, they will soon be coming right at you. You will have two or three diesels and the same number of submersibles if Brearly's helicopters and Trey's green waiting laser don't sink them. Sorry, I know that is a hand full. Watch for survivors and neutralize. Octavio, if the diesels come, try to lead them and drop the mines where their bows will slam onto the beach. If you miss, head on to the west end of the beach and see if Zulinda needs back-up. If not, hurry back and rake the diesels with automatic fire. Don't shoot any naked people. That should be plenty to sink them. Same treatment for survivors. Continue patrolling back and forth until I tell you to stand down."

"Roger that, Octavio, out."

"Vanna, sitrep?"

"Birdcage, one submersible tried to slip by. Trey hit it with green. I am 'shooting gallery' the others. One other diesel has a thug ducking and screaming. A suicide runs to our beach. Out of Trey's site-lines. Over."

"Vanna, you've got to stop him. Have the boat captain nail him with the other RPG. Follow in case he surfaces. Put Trey on your shooting gallery when he can get them in site."

Vanna barks, "Black Bird, do you see the suicide boat heading toward our dock?" Support please."

"Black Bird, on it. Now you see them, green laser, now you don't. Birdcage, some clean-up will be needed before your next clients hit the beach in the morning. Mukwonago left in time. Octavio has decimated any floating object near Zulinda. You can have your boat captains stand down but remain wary. Watch for stragglers."

'Thank you, Black Bird, much obliged. Out."

"Zulinda, Sitrep."

"Lance, all but one down. One got away into the woods, coming your way. God, could I use Bucky!"

Lance neutralizes the stray, then, "Vanna, could you get Trey down from the tower and our Boat Captain to help you get the bodies into the thug boats. Trey's unharmed, right? If you need more room, use our security boat. Tow them around the corner and north while we clean up here. We have so many, and a Don J. Mondo. They have an endless swamp of these treasonous bastards, as obsequious as our local thugs, sliming their way to the Autocratic top. We'll cover Octavio's deck for blood with a canvass for the Davy Jones Trip."

CHAPTER SEVENTY-FOUR

Starr's Loss, Fran's Future

Vanna updates "Trey's fine, looking sweaty and good enough to eat."

"Lover, save your appetite for me, I'm marinated."

Lance summarizes, "Black Bird, it's done with no injuries on our staff except Roberto with an embedded thorn. Cindy is at our resort and will be all over him."

"We have a full Valhalla load going soon. Any donations? Over"

"Birdcage, one of our guys got a 30-06 in the arm. He's patched up and will be fine. If I have extra refuse, my helicopter will follow your boat to the deep. Get some sleep now. Out"

CHAPTER SEVENTY-FIVE

205

Pedro Jet coasted to the end of the gravel runway of Guanaja. He turned into the wind, braked and jumped out of the pilot seat. He loaded the meager amount of passenger gear; circled around opening the passenger door. He pulled straps tight and went back to buckle himself in. Good wind, he raced.

As the wheels came up, Trey looked back, waved once at the staff waiting in the trees, turned ahead, and never looked back. This chapter, so beautiful, frightful, and maturing, was over. Next stop, Mukwonago, the Place of the Bear, pure joy.

END BOOK ONE

Follow the ensuing pleasures and horrors of Lance and Vanna with now Alicia and Laxmi, the Nepali security guard. Look for Guanaja Defense TWO and then move to Croatia in Book Guanaja, The Final Chapter.

BOOK TWO- EXCERPT

Vanna Richards orders: "Once again, ladies and gentlemen, this assault of theirs will start either early morning, or late evening. They will be forced to come by boat and will want to use light to camouflage their movements. We must keep them off shore for as long as possible. You start with rifles with regular ammo. Second clip should be tracers. Don't doubt for a second, they are here to kill us. You cannot hesitate" If you recognize their Donny J. Mondo, take him out immediately."

Lance, "Vanna, I'll go down and see what the boat captains are willing or able to do."

Roberto, Vanna and I had agreed that if this raid took place, and if we survived, we needed to take the fighting to them. Roberto had bought the shrimp fields and in closing received maps of all the lot lines on the island including the large castle. I flew the drone over the castle at altitude, and located the room large enough to hold their armaments and ammunition.

Vanna continues," Be reminded, we are dealing with a large group of murderous, greedy bastards, and we can't go in there and expect with our small numbers to neutralize them. From the pictures, I can place explosive charges that should combine with what they have in there and bring down that part of the fort. The drone is powerful enough to take what we need in two trips. Next time they come and we see them moving our way to attack, we send the first drone load as they leave their shore. Lance has technology to deliver the load right on target. The second load goes immediately to get the drone back to support the battle. We have an hour to prepare."

....
....

GUANAJA DEFENSE, SECOND EXCERPT, BOOK TWO

No sooner had I closed my eyes than the camp sea-radio ramped off. Octavio had actually had a date with a sharp girl, someone very special. He got the overnight invitation. When he returned to Gulfport the next day, two thug boats appeared, stalking him. He headed east and they would follow. West they would follow.

Lance, sleepy, "This is Birdcage, what's wrong Octavio?"

Lance paused, "Ok, Octavio, listen. Go back among the yachts. If you know anybody there, stay and chat. Don't get out of the breakwater."

"Hold on, Buddy!"

"Roberto, where are you?"

"I encouraged some shrimp relationship building and Cindy had a better idea. Why are you interrupting me?"

"Roberto, I'm sorry, my shame to Cindy, but listen to this conversation with Rayban in Gulfport:

From Lance, "How many thug boats are hunting you? Is there something they want on the boat, or will they steal the boat? Do you have the cash on board from the flounder sales?"

"Do you have armament? Octavio, keep that absolutely out of site. If the cops there see a big black guy with an RPG, I'll be hunting for bail money. Get a sound suppressed rifle with regular ammo."

"One Sec., I've got Roberto."

"Lance, I put all cash in a safe deposit in Gulfport for my lawyer Felipe to deal with. They are not going to take my boat over my dead body. I can out-run them. I got 23 knots to their seven."

"Octavio, Songbird, the U.S. Drone base said they cruise 18 knots with an empty boat. Roberto is on his way to me." Birdcage will come part of the way for you, only then do you make a run for us. Understood.? Only if they make a move to come inside the breakwater do you start shooting and running. Clear!"

"Well, you have always been right before. Put your boat in overdrive. I am sweating it here! Octavio, out."

www.ingramcontent.com/pod-product-compliance
Lightning Source LLC
Chambersburg PA
CBHW030137010826
48973CB00002B/605